WINTER'S DUTY

Talon Winter Legal Thriller #5

STEPHEN PENNER

D1235405

ISBN: 978-0-578-32757-0

Winter's Duty

This is a work of fiction. Any similarity with real persons or events is purely coincidental. Persons, events, and locations are either the product of the author's imagination or used fictitiously.

Joy Lorton, Editor.
Cover design by Nathan Wampler Book Covers.

WINTER'S
DUTY

A criminal defendant is entitled to the faithful and devoted services of his attorney, uninhibited by the dictates of conscience.

Johns v. Smyth,
United States District Court
176 F.Supp. 949 (E.D. Va. 1959)

CHAPTER 1

"What a loathsome piece of shit."

Talon Winter, attorney at law, defender of the accused, and speaker of her mind, pointed at the television and looked to her friend for confirmation. "Right?"

Patty Rodgers, also attorney at law, also defender of the accused, and never one to hedge her opinions just to make someone else happy, only shrugged. "I don't know. Innocent until proven guilty, right? I bet there's more to the story."

Talon frowned and turned back to the news broadcast. Her long black hair dropped angrily down her back, as if in solidarity with the frown and crossed arms. "Grandson murders grandparents with baseball bat," she recounted. "Sounds like a complete story to me."

"The murders have shocked the otherwise idyllic community of Gig Harbor," the newscaster continued. "Long known as a sleepy town of affluent professionals and active retirees, separated from the crime and turmoil of Tacoma by the short but symbolic drive over the Narrows Bridge, the coastal hamlet's residents feel a little less secure tonight."

Patty pointed at the T.V. this time. "Fancy language for a

local news report."

It was Talon's turn to shrug. "They probably have a creative writing major on their staff. What else are you going to do with that degree?"

Patty stood up and crossed to the counter on the other side of the communal break room in Talon's office building. She was a little bit older than Talon; a little bit shorter; a little bit heavier; with an ever-increasing number of stray gray hairs and deepening lines around her eyes, earned from a career of defending the worst people from the consequences of their worst actions. "You could go to law school," she suggested. "More pad thai?"

"Of course," Talon answered, in reference to the pad thai. "Is that what you did? Were you a creative writing major?"

Patty picked up the entire container of food and carried it back to the couch she and Talon were seated on. "No, I was an English major. It was a lot easier critiquing other people's writing than trying to write anything myself."

Talon nodded. "I think a lot of life is like that." She jerked a thumb at the television. "Whoever gets that case is going to attack everything from the crime scene investigation to the DNA analysis."

"If they bother to do any DNA analysis," Patty said through a half-full mouth of noodles. "Sounds like they caught him at the scene with the bloody bat in his hands. You don't need DNA analysis for that."

"Might have been someone else's blood on the bat," Talon argued deadpan. "Should have tested it."

"A reasonable doubt may arise from the evidence or the lack of evidence," Patty recited the language from the standard jury instruction with a laugh. "If they didn't test the bat, you must acquit."

Talon shook her head and swallowed her bite. "Doesn't

rhyme."

"Does it have to rhyme?" Patty asked.

"It would have rhymed if you'd been a creative writing major," Talon teased.

"What would have rhymed?" asked Curt Fairchild, private investigator to the defense bar, acquaintance to Patty Rodgers, and failed but still hopeful lover to Talon, as he walked into the break room. "Ooh, is that pad thai?"

"Yes," Talon answered, "and no, you can't have any."

"There should be some fried rice left," Patty offered.

"Don't encourage him," Talon chided. "The worst thing you can do is encourage him."

Curt filled a paper plate with what was left of the fried rice—mostly large cucumber slices and limp onion tendrils—and sat down in the chair next to Talon's side of the couch. He was dressed in his usual work attire: khakis and a polo that showed off his biceps. And pecs. Talon looked away, after a moment.

"What would have rhymed?" Curt repeated his question.

Talon rolled her eyes. "Nothing, Curt. You walked in at the end of a conversation."

Patty nodded toward the television. "We were talking about that dude who murdered his grandparents. We were saying if they don't test the bat for DNA, that would be reasonable doubt."

"The bat covered in his grandparents' blood," Talon expounded.

Curt thought for a moment, then swallowed his mouthful of cucumber with rice. "Don't test the blood on the floor, my client walks out the door."

Patty grinned. "Hey, that's pretty good actually."

Talon shook her head. "Don't encourage him," she repeated. "And besides, the blood was on the bat."

"I bet it was on the floor, too," Curt muttered as he took another bite of rice and cucumber.

Patty shook her head. "What a terrible way to die."

"Eh." Talon shrugged. "We all die."

"That's pretty dark," Patty protested.

"It's not dark, it's true," Talon replied. "Each of us is born alone and each of us will die alone."

"Actually, we aren't born alone," Curt said. "By definition, being born means coming out of another person. Every one of us is specifically not alone when we're born."

"Whatever," Talon waved away the technicality. "Life is suffering. Death is inevitable. Life has no meaning."

"Again, dark," Patty said. "And sad. I hope life has meaning."

"It doesn't," Talon assured her.

"So, you make your own meaning," Curt suggested.

Talon rolled her eyes at that.

Patty frowned. "Did you know criminal defense attorneys have one of the highest suicide rates of any profession? Us and dentists. It's because everyone hates us. And dentists."

"They hate until they need us." Talon gestured at the television again. "Grandma and grandpa had a pretty nice house. Some defense attorney's gonna get a fat payday."

"Well, not from junior," Patty opined. "I'm pretty sure you don't get to inherit from the will if you're the one who killed grandpa."

"Maybe life insurance, though," Curt piped in.

"You can't collect life insurance if you murder the insured, Curt." Talon rolled her eyes.

"I don't know." Curt held a forkful of rice in front of his mouth. "I bet it depends on the policy. You didn't used to be able to collect if the person committed suicide, but now you can on a lot of policies."

"Really?" Patty asked.

"Encourage him," Talon reminded her friend. "Don't."

Patty hesitated, then acquiesced. She turned her attention back to the news report. "Well, that's going to be a huge case for whoever gets it. Two victims, wall-to-wall media coverage..."

"Blood-covered baseball bat," Curt added.

"Right," Patty said. "And they're going to put their best prosecutors on it. Probably O'Brien. Did I tell you I've got a case against O'Brien? Fucked up case, too. This guy comes home—"

But before she could finish recounting the facts of her case, Riley Watterson, the receptionist for the building, stuck her head into the break room.

"Ms. Winter? There's a call for you."

"It's after five," Talon responded. "It better be new business."

"Oh, it's new business, all right," Riley confirmed. She pointed at the television. "It's that asshole's mom and dad. They want to hire you."

CHAPTER 2

'New business'. That was the phrase every criminal defense attorney knew and loved and built their lives around. Defendants came and defendants went, cases were won and cases were lost, but on the first of the month the rent was due regardless. Law and justice and all that were fine and dandy, but you couldn't defend the accused on an empty stomach. Well, you could, but you didn't want to. You wanted a nice dinner and a comfortable place to lay your head at night. You wanted to get paid. You wanted to make money, and as much as possible. You wanted the retainers to keep filling up that small business account you set up when you took that leap of faith and struck out as a solo practitioner, dedicated to truth, justice, and the almighty dollar. You wanted new business.

But that new business might not want you. Sure, they called. They set up an appointment. They even showed up for the appointment. But you needed to close the deal. It was one thing to dial a number and schedule a consultation. It was another to hand over a credit card to someone you just met and have it handed back, maxed out, with more payments on the horizon. Defending a murder case wasn't cheap. And Talon Winter wasn't apologizing.

She was aware what she was asking. Give me your trust, and a whole lot of money. She needed to make that as easy as possible for them. They needed to trust her. They needed to be impressed by her. They needed to think she would be as competent and as professional and as awesome with the judge and jury as she was in that initial consultation. First impressions were everything.

That was why she opted for the sleek and spacious conference room with the view of Commencement Bay, rather than the cramped and cluttered confines of her office. She wasn't one of those psychos who somehow managed to keep a clean desk. She worked for a living. And her work was strewn about the office as it needed to be for whatever cases she was working on at that particular moment. Talon felt it radiated hard work, but she understood it could come across as overworked, or worse, overwhelmed. It was better to be calm, cool, collected, and in the conference room when Karen and Chad Burgess arrived for their free initial consultation, which they did five minutes early.

Talon liked that. She didn't expect to like much else, though. At least not until that credit card got handed over. After all, little Johnny Burgess was a loathsome piece of shit.

Riley brought Mr. and Mrs. Burgess to the conference room where Talon was already decamped and waiting. She made sure to have her back to the windows so they would have the view of the water. Speaking of water, there were two glasses of water already poured for them, and as they entered and approached their seats, Riley made sure to ask, as Talon had instructed, "Would you like any coffee or tea?"

Karen Burgess let out a small gasp. "What? Oh, no. No, thank you. No, I don't think so. Do you want any coffee, Chad?"

Chad shook his head. "No, thank you, miss," he said to Riley. "I'm sure we'll be fine with just water."

They were the paradigm of a successful middle-class couple, somewhere in their early 40s, but trying to hang on to their late 30s.

Karen had long, bleached blonde hair and a lot of dangly jewelry. Chad had sunglasses hanging on a strap on top of a pastel polo shirt that only drew attention to the tan he had over-cultivated despite his pale skin. They both had perfectly straight, overly whitened teeth.

As Riley closed the door to the conference room behind her, Chad extended a hand across the table. "Miss Winter. Thank you for meeting with us."

"Ms.," Talon corrected as she shook his hand. "And of course. It sounds like your son has gotten himself into a whole lot of trouble."

That sounded better than, 'Your son is a psychotic murderer'. It also immediately framed the conversation around the consequences he was facing, rather than what he did. And how Talon might be able to help him avoid those consequences.

Karen choked back a sob. "He sure has. Oh dear, he sure has. Hasn't he, Chad?"

Chad reached over and patted his wife's hand. "He sure has, honey. He sure has." He looked to Talon. "Do you think you can help him, Miss Winter?"

Talon took a moment as she decided whether to correct Chad again about the whole 'Miss' versus 'Ms.' thing, or ignore it and push forward toward that credit card at the end of the meeting.

Karen jumped into the pause. "He couldn't have done what they're saying he did, Miss Winter. My parents loved him so much. He just couldn't have done it."

Talon was going to have to ignore the 'Miss'. She couldn't let it take over the consultation.

Chad patted Karen's hand again. "Well, I'm sure the police are doing their jobs very well, dear, but there's probably more to it. Doesn't that sound right, Miss Winter? There's got to be more to it, right?"

"Right," Talon agreed. "There's always more to it. What you're hearing right now is only one part of the story. The first part. The simple part. The easy part. But things like this aren't simple and they aren't easy. There's more to this. I know that already. And it's in that more that we'll find a way to help your son."

Karen gasped again and squeezed her husband's hand. "You see, dear? I told you she'd understand. I just knew you would understand."

Talon understood alright. She understood these parents were never going to be able to accept what their child had done. She wasn't being hired to defend him just in court. She was being hired to defend him in their eyes as well. But Talon didn't mind. It was all included in the fee.

Talon knew she was in sales. Selling plea bargains to prosecutors. Selling acquittals to juries. And perhaps most importantly, selling hope and compassion to defendants. Or their parents. Especially their parents. It was a delicate balance. She had to keep them hopeful enough to think it was worth it to hire an attorney. But she was mindful of that old advice: under-promise and over-deliver. She needed the Burgesses to have hope, but she also needed them to be primed for some of the realities their son was facing after beating his grandparents to death with a goddamn baseball bat.

"Let's talk a little bit more about your son," she directed, "and what he's facing."

"Yes, let's do that," Karen quickly agreed. She made a motion at her husband who somehow knew that meant to pull out his wallet. While he did that, Karen continued. "Once you know more about him, you'll see, he really is a very good boy."

Talon considered the pools of blood she hoped the police

would forget to test and offered her most sincere fake smile. "I'm sure he is, Mrs. Burgess. I'm sure he is."

CHAPTER 3

It turned out that the Burgesses' little boy wasn't named Johnny. He was named Hunter. Even worse.

He wasn't a little boy either. He was a grown man, handsome and tall, with a strong jaw, sandy hair, and blue eyes Talon expected to be tinged with a touch of crazy. But there wasn't any crazy there. Just calm and confidence. Which, given what everyone knew he'd done, was also worse. A lot worse.

They met in one of the mostly private attorney-client conference rooms inside the Pierce County Jail. 'Mostly' because a guard was still watching through the reinforced glass window in the door. He wouldn't listen in on the legally privileged conversation, but he wasn't going to take his eyes off an inmate either. Especially not an accused murderer. Especially not that murder. Murders.

"Good morning, Hunter," Talon started the conversation. "My name is Talon Winter. Your parents hired me yesterday to represent you. You're going to be arraigned on two counts of murder in the first degree this afternoon, and I'm going to be your lawyer."

Hunter Burgess took a moment, then asked, "Why you?"

Talon had her answer ready. "Because I'm the best."

Hunter narrowed his eyes. "We'll see." Then, after another moment of consideration, "I'm going to need the best, huh?"

Talon returned his nod. "You sure are."

"Okay." Hunter smiled. "Sounds like fun."

'Fun'. Talon could already tell it wasn't going to be fun.

"My parents hired you?" Hunter asked with a chuckle. "Aren't they upset? Especially my mom. It was her parents."

"Yes, Hunter," Talon answered. "They're both very upset. And I can hardly blame them. But their immediate concern seems to be you."

Hunter grinned again and leaned back smugly into the flimsy plastic chair the jail provided inmates who might be tempted to turn furniture into weapons. "I knew it. I knew they would put me first. That's what parents are supposed to do. Put me first."

Talon was starting to see what might have led to the fact pattern of her latest case.

"So, what do we do now?" Hunter asked. "Do you want me to tell you how I did it?"

"No." Talon had that answer ready, too. And for two reasons. One, she was already getting bad vibes from Hunter Burgess. She didn't think she would enjoy his recitation of the murders. But two, and more importantly, she explained, "I don't need to hear it from you. I don't need to know what actually happened. Not yet anyway. I need to hear it from them, not you. I need to read the police reports. I need to know what they think happened. Because that's what I need to defend against. If they messed it up—and they usually mess it up—I want to be able to see that clearly without having your more accurate version of events in my brain. Does that make sense?"

It didn't really matter if it made sense to him, but if it did, then she could more easily move on to the more pressing matter of his impending arraignment.

Hunter frowned slightly. He clearly wanted to describe to her what he'd done to his mother's parents, with all of the very literally gory details. He crossed his arms. "I guess so," he pouted.

"Good." Talon was glad to accept the response. "Let's talk about what's going to happen next."

Hunter shrugged. "What's going to happen next?"

"You're going to be arraigned," Talon explained, "and then the judge is going to set bail."

Hunter's expression lit up again. "I'm going to get out?"

"No." Talon shook her head. "The judge is going to set your bail so high you can't get out."

"My parents have a lot of money." Hunter was hopeful.

Not after they get done paying me to represent your homicidal ass, thought Talon. Instead, she said, "The judge will take that into account. You don't murder two people and get to walk out the door to await trial."

Hunter leaned forward and opened those blue, not crazy eyes wide. "You think I did it?"

Talon didn't have an answer ready for that. But it didn't matter.

Hunter laughed and waved his own question away. "Nah, I'm just messing with you. I totally did it. But we're gonna win anyway, right? Because you're the best, right?"

"Yes," Talon sighed. "I'm the best."

CHAPTER 4

Being the best had its limits, however, without also having power. Even the best ant would still get squashed by the worst boot.

In the criminal justice system, Talon was the ant. The boot was the prosecutor. And the boot assigned to Hunter Burgess's case was anything but the worst boot. He was the top boot. The boss boot. The Chief of the Criminal Division boot. The second-in-command to the Elected D.A. boot. The boot's name was Ron Riordan and Talon knew he was handling her case as soon as he walked into the crowded arraignment courtroom three minutes before the judge was scheduled to take the bench. That was mainly because he never came to court anymore, so if he was coming for any case, it would be the slam dunk double homicide that had been on the news nonstop since grandma and grandpa were found soaking in pools of their own blood.

Riordan had tried every big case that office had seen for over a decade before eventually settling into the day-to-day management of the criminal division of the county attorney's office. He was the equivalent of hand sewn, albino crocodile skin boots, with alpaca fur lining and twenty karat gold spurs. Talon's only hope was that the boots had been up on the shelf just a little too long, and the dust was just a little too deep in the cracks of the alligator skin to be wiped completely away for one last night on the town.

Still, they were nice boots. Riordan was in his early fifties, but had clearly made the decision to fight against time and stay in shape rather than give in quite yet to the inevitable physical decline age brought to everyone eventually. He was tall and trim, with broad shoulders and a flat stomach, and more than a little gray in his perfectly styled black hair. No glasses to hide the wrinkles around his eyes, but those lines made him look wise, even rugged, not old.

Talon frowned. The jury was going to love him. Especially the middle-aged women. She had already been thinking about the composition of the jury she would need to pull a rabbit out of Grandpa Burgess's blood-soaked top hat. She was thinking moms, with kids about Hunter's age. But those were exactly the people who would be charmed by the handsome older man in the athletic-cut suit, standing before them seeking justice for the victims who were probably just about the age of those jurors' parents.

Riordan had presence. It was on display as every other prosecutor in the courtroom scurried out of their boss's way when he approached the lower bench and advised the clerk, quite unnecessarily, "I'm here on the Burgess matter."

Talon stepped up as well. She was no scurrier. "I'm here on that case as well. Talon Winter for the defense."

Riordan turned to greet her. "Ms. Winter, was it? I don't believe we've met before." He extended his hand. "I'm Ron Riordan."

Talon shook his hand. "Nice to finally meet you in person, Mr. Riordan. So, they sent the big guns for this one, huh?"

Riordan smiled. "I sent myself. This is an important case. And anyway, I've been itching to get back into the courtroom."

"And in front of the cameras." Talon nodded toward the row of television cameras in the back of the courtroom. "I heard your boss may not run for reelection again. Are you eyeing the top job, Mr. Riordan?"

Prosecutors were all holier-than-thou. It was a job requirement. How could you send people to rot in cages for years of their lives unless you thought you were better than them? So, first thing to do was to question his motives. Better yet, make him question his own motives.

But he hadn't made his way up to the number two job because he was easily rattled. He grinned. "I'm just here to see to it that justice is done."

Talon returned the grin. "How about that? Me too."

Further conversation was preempted by the entrance of the judge.

"All rise!" called the bailiff. "The Pierce County Superior Court is now in session, The Honorable Stacy Holdbrook presiding."

Talon relaxed a little. Holdbrook was a good judge. She'd been a civil litigator before ascending to the bench. It took her a while to get her hands around the criminal cases, but she managed it, and she didn't bring with her any of the bias of being a former prosecutor. She would be fair. Unfortunately, Talon knew 'fair' would mean a very high bail. Presumed innocent or not, you don't release the guy who beat his own grandparents to death with a baseball bat.

"Mr. Riordan." Judge Holdbrook recognized him. She was elected too. There was a whole stratum of political movers and shakers that cut across the heart of the criminal justice system. It was kind of gross, actually. In Talon's humble opinion anyway. "To what do we owe the honor of you descending from your office into our humble courtroom?"

Talon fought back a sickened grimace. Her opinion of Judge Holdbrook was threatening to decline.

"It's a privilege to be in your courtroom, Your Honor," Riordan returned with his own winning smile. "I am here to represent the State in the matter of *The State of Washington versus Hunter Burgess.*"

Judge Holdbrook offered the slightest of smiles herself. "I suspected as much when I saw you. Is that matter ready?"

"It is, Your Honor," Riordan answered.

"The defense is ready as well, Your Honor," Talon spoke up. "Talon Winter, appearing on behalf of Mr. Burgess."

Judge Holdbrook turned her gaze briefly to Talon. "Ah, Ms. Winter. Good to see you as well." Then back to the prosecutor. "You may call the case, Mr. Riordan."

It could be hard to notice the ant through the glare from the million-dollar boot.

Riordan formally announced the case and the jail guard stationed at the door to the holding cells pulled it open with a clank to shout, "Burgess!" into the void. A few moments later, Hunter emerged, dressed in red jail jammies, handcuffed to belly chains, and absolutely beaming as he surveyed the room full of people who had come to see him.

Those middle-aged women jurors were going to hate him if Talon didn't teach him to look a little bit contrite, maybe even sad. Not like he'd just walked into his own birthday party.

The jailer pushed Burgess into place next to Talon.

"Hello, Ms. Winter," he said in not at all a whisper. "It's good to see you again."

But Talon hushed him. "Don't say anything. Pay attention to the judge and let me do the talking."

"Yes, Ms. Winter." And he raised his eyes to Judge Holdbrook. At least he was compliant. So far.

"This is the matter of *The State of Washington versus Hunter Archer Burgess,*" Judge Holdbrook declared formally. "The State has filed a criminal complaint against Mr. Burgess charging him with two counts of murder in the first degree. Has the defense received copies of the complaint?"

Riordan slid two copies of the complaint to Talon even as the judge was asking the question. It was three pages long. Talon's copy was stapled. The copy for Burgess had no staple, lest he shove it in a guard's eye. The prosecutor always did that, and Talon always thought it was silly. Until then.

"Yes, Your Honor," Talon answered. Then, the standard recitation: "The defense would acknowledge receipt of the complaint, waive a formal reading of the charges, and ask the Court to enter pleas of not guilty to all charges."

"Pleas of not guilty will be entered," the judge ordered. Then it was time for the bail argument. "I will hear first from the State regarding conditions of release."

Of course. The prosecutor always went first, even at trial. But there were advantages to hearing all of the other side's arguments and evidence before making your pitch. Talon knew how to make that an advantage at trial. She also knew it wasn't going to matter at all at the bail hearing.

"The State would ask the Court to set bail at two million dollars," Riordan requested, "on each count, for a total of four million dollars. When setting bail, the Court should consider the risk of flight and the safety of the community. If convicted as charged, the defendant is facing life in prison without the possibility of parole. There could be no greater incentive to flee. Furthermore, the defendant is accused of murdering his own grandparents, and in a terrible, gruesome way. If his own grandparents weren't safe from him, then I would submit, Your Honor, none of us are. Thank you."

Judge Holdbrook nodded along to everything Riordan said, then turned to Talon, even if only because she was required to hear from both sides before giving the prosecutor whatever he asked for. "Any argument, Ms. Winter?"

A lawyer's reputation was everything. It preceded her, and in so doing, already affected the listener before she uttered a word. One built a reputation over time, case by case, issue by issue, argument by argument. The judges learned whom they could believe and who was blowing smoke up their black-robed asses. Most lawyers would concede arguments they knew they would lose in order to maintain, even build, credibility for later when they argued an issue they might actually win, even if it was a different case for a different client. Talon wasn't most lawyers. And that wasn't her reputation.

"Yes, Your Honor," she said. Of course. "The prosecutor's request is excessive, Your Honor, bordering on ridiculous, and his reasoning is even worse. The court rule governing bail, rule 3.2, states clearly and unequivocally that in all cases, not just misdemeanors or low-level property crimes, but in all cases, a release on personal recognizance is presumed. Presumed. That means, absent compelling evidence put forward by the prosecution, a criminal defendant should be released from custody pending the outcome of his trial, which only makes sense if we are to take the constitutionally enshrined presumption of innocence seriously. Even then, the prosecution can't just come in and argue any old reasons to hold a constitutionally innocent person in jail. The arguments they make and the evidence they present must be directed to two, and only two factors. Is there any reason to believe the defendant will not appear for future court dates? And is there any reason to believe the defendant poses a risk to the safety of a particular person or the community as a whole? Absent evidence to support a finding of the existence of these factors, a court must allow a defendant to remain out of custody pending his trial."

Talon gestured at Riordan, but didn't look at him directly. Still, she could see out of the corner of her eye that he had crossed his arms and was looking incredulously at her. *Good.*

"Now, the State would have you believe that the charges themselves are sufficient evidence of those factors, that the potential penalty and the factual allegations inherent in a murder case would authorize setting of bail, and indeed astronomically high bail. But that cannot be the case. It simply cannot. Because every charge of murder in the first degree carries with it a decades-long prison sentence. And every charge of murder in the first degree involves an allegation that the defendant acted in a violent and unjustifiable way. But if it were true that every murder case met the requirements for a court to require bail, then the rule itself would say so. Certainly, when they drafted the court rules, the State Supreme Court, in its wisdom, knew how to write, 'Except in cases of first-degree murder, a release on personal recognizance is presumed.' Of course, they knew how to write that. And of course, they did not. Even in murder cases, even in cases involving multiple charges of first-degree murder, a personal recognizance release is presumed. And not just presumed, Your Honor, but required. Unless the prosecution can present evidence why it shouldn't be."

Talon glanced at Riordan then, but only so she could do so dismissively.

"And what evidence did they present? Why, absolutely none at all. All they did was march in their Chief of the Criminal Division, with his lengthy resume and his shiny suit, who offered his personal observation that the punishment for murder sure is a lot, and his personal and entirely unsupported speculation that someone who is accused of hurting someone they know must also be capable of hurting any one of us at any time for no apparent reason."

Talon shook her head and looked back up to Judge Holdbrook. "Well, that's not how it works. That's not how any of this works. We have rules for a reason. We have laws for a reason. And I cannot understand how a man who makes his living not only enforcing rules against others, but also supervises and directs all of the prosecutors in this county who make their livings enforcing rules against others, can walk into this courtroom and ask this Court to ignore those rules when it suits him.

"If he truly respected the rule of law he claims to uphold, then he would have come into this court and given Your Honor actual evidence to support his request. Instead, he has shown his contempt for those rules and invited the Court to share and approve of his disdain for our carefully balanced and intentionally calibrated system of criminal justice."

Another wave toward Riordan. But again, no actual glance at her opponent.

"Decline that invitation, Your Honor. Reject arguments without evidence. Uphold the rule of law as promulgated by the highest court of this state. Do justice. Release my client. Thank you."

There was a certain charge in the courtroom as all of the other lawyers had ceased their side conversations to listen to the defense attorney who had just called out the Chief Criminal Prosecutor and dared the judge to release her double murder defendant.

But Talon knew better, despite her rule-based argument.

"Thank you for your advocacy, Ms. Winter," Judge

CHAPTER 5

Hunter somehow seemed both surprised and nonplussed by Judge Holdbrook's bail ruling.

"I hope you're still the best," he told her as the guard dragged him back toward the holding cells.

Riordan seemed less appreciative. He stormed out of the courtroom as soon as the judge announced her ruling.

"Ron!" Talon called after him as he exited through the back of the courtroom. She caught up to him in the hallway outside. "Ron, do you have a minute to chat about the case? I'd love to see where your head is at on this one."

'Ron' wasn't having it. Not only were prosecutors well known to be holier-than-thou, they were also notoriously thin skinned.

"I'll tell you where my head is at, Ms. Winter," he growled. "You just accused me of violating the law."

Talon raised a finger. "Actually, I accused you of asking the judge to violate the law. Which she did, by the way."

"I don't appreciate being accused of that either," Riordan said through clenched teeth.

Talon shrugged. "Then next time bring evidence instead of

just your opinion."

Riordan's eyes narrowed. "I'd heard of your reputation, Ms. Winter. I wasn't sure I believed it until now."

"It's true. I advocate zealously for my clients," she admitted. "Now, do you want to discuss the case or not?"

"I'll choose 'not'," Riordan replied. "At least not right now. I need to get back to my office and continue my nefarious schemes to violate your client's rights and the rights of everyone we've charged with a crime."

"I know you think you're joking," Talon pointed at him, "but that is kind of what you do. Or at least what you would do if it weren't for zealous advocates like me."

"Don't presume to tell me what I would do," Riordan warned.

"No need to presume," Talon countered. "We both just witnessed it. I'll see you at the pretrial conference then. Don't say I didn't warn you."

Riordan frowned at Talon's last comment. He didn't seem to know whether it was a threat, a further criticism, or a *non sequitur*. Just as Talon intended. She turned and walked away, leaving him to contemplate why he felt like he just lost a hearing he'd won.

And Talon got to feel like she'd won a hearing she'd definitely lost.

Karen Burgess rushed up to her and gave her a hug. Talon was not a fan of hugs. But she was a fan of large retainers and prepaid fees. She managed a single pat on Karen's back before her client's mother released her and his father stepped up, hands in his pockets, but a grateful smile on his face. "That was very impressive, Miss Winter. I knew we hired the right attorney."

Talon declined to point out that the judge set bail exactly as the prosecutor asked. It wasn't about that. It was about being the lawyer who made those arguments anyway. It was about her reputation. After all, it was that reputation that had led the Burgess family to call her in the first place.

"Thank you," Talon offered, "but this was just the beginning of what is going to be a very long, very arduous journey to get a good result for you and your son."

Karen's smile melted into a frown. "What's next then?"

"Next," Talon answered, "I have a lot of reading to do."

Karen's frown only deepened.

"The police reports," Talon explained. "Thousands of pages of police reports."

"Oh," Karen responded. "That doesn't sound like very much fun."

"This job isn't fun, Ms. Burgess," Talon answered. "But it's important."

CHAPTER 6

Reading the police reports was necessary, but it wasn't sufficient. And it wasn't the truly fun part. Accumulation of information was required. It was the processing of that information that was interesting. Throw in a team to go over that information and another delivery from the Thai place up the road, and it could almost be fun. In a dark, 'two people were murdered by their own grandson' sort of way.

The team was the same as when Talon had gotten the call from Mr. and Mrs. We Don't Care What Our Little Boy Did We Still Love Him, plus a couple of hangers-on who weren't directly involved in the practice of law but who nevertheless worked in the same building and also were fans of the aforementioned Thai restaurant up the road. Talon had invited Patty and Curt to join her. Riley the receptionist and Paul Delgado had invited themselves when Paul, the de facto building manager with the ill-defined day job, walked by the conference room and overheard Talon asking Patty if she wanted to add some spring rolls to the order. Twenty minutes later, lunch was delivered and Talon had the floor.

"The key to any successful defense in a criminal case," she began, "is a credible counter narrative. One that accepts the facts presented by the prosecution but repackages them to fit into a different story that's consistent with innocence."

"Can you do that with this case?" Patty asked. "Now that you've seen the police reports?"

"No," Talon answered. "No, I cannot."

"Not much of a strategy session then," Paul observed. He was the dark and stocky type, with thick black hair and a neatly trimmed goatee. He claimed to work in data collection but was never willing to disclose the exact nature of the data, the process of collection, or the identity of his clients. He was confident, even cocky, and smart. Talon didn't trust him, but she was more than willing to use him.

"Not yet," Talon clarified. "If I had my counter narrative already, you'd be eating by yourself right now."

Paul grinned. "I doubt that."

Patty rolled her eyes and tried to get the conversation back on a professional track. "Mental health defense?" she suggested.

Talon shook her head. "I don't want to go that route. Not unless I absolutely have to. A mental health defense means admitting he did it but trying to explain why. Best case scenario is he spends the rest of his life in a mental hospital instead of prison. Either way, that's a loss."

"Maybe that's where he belongs," Curt suggested. "I mean, you have to be crazy to murder your own grandparents, don't you?"

"Depends on your grandparents," Riley put in. She was 'just' the receptionist, but Talon hoped she might provide the viewpoint of the average citizen juror. At least, that was how she consoled herself when Riley stuck her head into the conference room and also agreed they should order spring rolls and also a round of Thai iced teas. "My grandpa was a fucking asshole."

"'He deserved it' isn't a great defense either," Talon said, "although I have used it in the past."

"Did it work?" Patty asked.

"Let's just focus on this case," Talon non-answered. "The problem with that defense is that it also admits the crime. 'He did it, but it's okay.' I want something where he didn't do it."

"But he did, right?" Curt asked. "He did beat his grandparents to death with a baseball bat, right?"

"That's not really the point," Patty jumped in. "That's the prosecution's job to prove. Talon's job is to create reasonable doubt in the state's case."

"It needs to be more than that," Talon said. "It's not enough to cast doubt in their story. It has to be a different story that can stand on its own."

"But isn't that harder if he's actually guilty?" Curt insisted. "If he actually did it?"

"Well, he didn't confess to it," Talon said. "He was smart enough to lawyer up when the cops arrested him."

"That's good," Patty confirmed.

"But," Talon continued, "they arrested him inside the home, holding the bat, and covered in blood."

Curt looked over at Patty. "That's bad."

"That's one of those facts I can't change," Talon conceded. "I just need to be able to explain it."

"How do you explain something like that?" Curt asked.

Talon nodded back at him. "How would you explain it, Curt?"

"Me?" He put a hand to his chest. "Why me?"

"Because you obviously think he's guilty," Paul knew. "So, something that could convince you he's innocent is the best scenario to convince the jury." He looked to Talon for confirmation. "Right?"

Talon smiled. Paul had earned his pad thai. "Right."

Curt frowned and thought for a moment. "Okay," he finally said. "What about this? He didn't kill them, but he did find the bodies. He got blood on himself because he tried to resuscitate them. And he was holding the bat because he found it there, and he didn't want the real killer to come back and use it against him."

"Shit, that's almost believable," Patty commended. "Good job."

"So, who did do it then?" Talon asked.

"Are you asking me?" Curt responded.

"Yes," Talon confirmed. "It's your story."

Curt frowned again. "I don't know. Burglars maybe? Someone you wouldn't be able to find so they can't refute the story."

"Wrong," Paul chimed in again. "No one will believe that. It's too convenient. It needs to be someone the jury won't believe when they do deny it."

"Or someone who won't deny it," Talon added. That counter narrative was starting to come together in her head.

"Who wouldn't deny a double homicide they didn't commit?" Curt threw his hands up.

"Don't worry," Talon said. "I'll figure that out next."

She nodded to herself and allowed a faint grin to unfurl in one corner of her mouth. "You know," she mused, "if I do this right, I might just be able to combine 'my guy's crazy', 'the victim deserved it', and 'it wasn't me' into one big fat 'not guilty' verdict."

A murmur of affirmation circled the room. Then Patty raised her fork and said, "This reminds me of one of my own cases that I have coming up for trial. My guy—"

But before she could say more there was a knock on the doorframe of the conference room entrance.

"Sorry to interrupt," said the tall woman with the long

blonde hair and the expertly tailored business suit, "but there was no one at the front desk. Could someone tell me where I could find a Ms. Talon Winter?"

CHAPTER 7

Talon set her fork down and stood to greet her unknown visitor. The woman had an air of The System about her. Talon's guard went up.

"I'm Talon Winter," she announced.

"Oh!" the woman exclaimed. She was younger than her attire would have suggested. "Oh yes. Of course you are. Hello. I'm Cassandra Sondheim, of Erickson, Larson and Sondheim."

"Is that a law firm?" Patty asked without standing up herself.

Cassandra Sondheim smirked reflexively at the question. "Um, yes. We're one of the biggest civil litigation firms in Seattle."

"This is Tacoma," Talon pointed out.

"Yes, exactly," Cassandra said. "That's why I've come, Ms. Winter. I have a proposition for you."

"Sounds dirty," Paul only half-whispered.

Talon shot him a look. "Perhaps we should go to my office," she suggested. "We were done here anyway."

"Oh, okay," Patty said.

"Can we at least finish our food?" Curt complained.

"I guess I better get back to my desk," Riley stood up with

her takeout tray, "before some other random stranger appears to proposition someone."

"Send them to my office," Paul said.

"What if it's a dude?" Riley teased.

Paul pursed his lips and stared at the ceiling for a long moment. "Them too. I can always be persuaded."

Talon stepped around the conference table and apologized for the others. "My office is just upstairs."

Once they were seated in that upstairs office, Talon got right to the point. Or rather she invited Cassandra Sondheim to get right to her point.

"So, what's your proposition, Ms. Sondheim? Are you looking for someone to refer white collar criminal cases to in exchange for divorce referrals? I'm not sure your firm would like my usual clientele, if they could even afford you."

"Um, no. Nothing like that." Cassandra cleared her throat. "As I said, Erickson, Larson and Sondheim is one of Seattle's premiere civil litigation firms—"

"Congratulations on that, by the way," Talon interjected. "And congrats on being one of the partners in the firm name. Nice to see a woman killing it like that."

"Oh, well, thanks," Cassandra shifted slightly in her seat, "but that Sondheim was actually my grandfather. He helped found the firm before I was even born."

"Ah." Talon leaned back in her chair. "So, I'm sorry, what's your proposal again? Not to be rude, but I have a lot of work to do for clients whose literal lives are in my hands."

Cassandra pulled on a sharp smile to cut through Talon's unconcealed skepticism. "Right to business. I like that. That's what my sources said about you and that's why I'm here."

Talon narrowed her eyes. "What sources?"

Cassandra avoided the question. "We are expanding our firm and about to open a Tacoma office. We want you to head up our office here."

"Me?"

"You."

"Here?"

"Tacoma. Yes."

Talon leaned even further back in her chair and steepled her fingers for a few moments. "Me?" she repeated.

Cassandra laughed lightly. "Yes, you. Of course you."

"Why of course me?" Talon questioned. "Those sources?"

"Yes." Cassandra nodded. "Those sources."

"The sources that you won't tell me who they are?" Talon tried again.

"We promise confidentiality when we research lawyers to approach about joining our firm," Cassandra explained. "It's the only way we can be sure to get honest appraisals. And we need accurate information if we are going to add someone to our team."

"And what was the information you got about me?" Talon asked. "What would make you show up here unannounced and offer me a job running the new Tacoma office of Whoever, Whoever, and Sondheim?"

"Simple," Cassandra answered with a smile. "You're the best."

CHAPTER 8

Talon was flattered. She was also suspicious. And truthfully, she was also too busy right then taking care of her existing clients to spend too much time considering abandoning all of them at the whim of Grandpa Sondheim's perfect Barbie doll of a granddaughter.

But she didn't say no either.

When opportunity knocks, you don't always have to open the door, but you don't lock the deadbolt either. She told Cassandra she'd think about it, and they scheduled a coffee for the following week. Talon explained she had some pressing matters she simply had to focus on. Chief among those was the pretrial conference on Hunter Burgess's case. Riordan could refuse to talk to her in the hallway after she'd embarrassed him in court, but he had to speak to her at the pretrial conference, if only because she'd move to dismiss if he didn't show up. It would never be granted, but he'd have to file a response, and she'd have another chance to school him in front of his subordinates at oral argument. Easier to just grit his teeth and come to the negotiating table with a positive attitude and an offer for two counts of first-degree manslaughter and a sentence under five years. That would be a win for Talon. It was also a pipe dream.

Although when Riordan walked into The Pit—the large conference room where all the prosecutors and defense attorneys showed up to negotiate their cases—he was smiling again. So, he had a positive attitude anyway. One out of two wasn't bad. He was faking it, of course, but two could play at that game.

"Ron!" Talon called out with a smile and a wave. "Over here. I grabbed us a table."

The joke was that she didn't have to save them a table. Riordan was literally the boss of every prosecutor in that overfilled room. They would be tripping over themselves to offer up their seat to the Chief of the Criminal Division.

Riordan took a moment to locate where the voice had come from, then his fake smile broadened, and he hurried over to join her at what she had set up to feel like 'her' table. Everything mattered and everything was intentional.

"So, I don't suppose you're going to offer to reduce the charges to manslaughter?" Talon led off the negotiations. No ask, no get.

Riordan's smile abided. "You know I can't do that, Ms. Winter."

"Call me Talon," she told him. "I'm sure as hell not going to call you 'Mr. Riordan'. I don't work for you."

"No, you do not," Riordan agreed. "I don't suppose your client is willing to plead guilty as charged to two counts of murder in the first degree, is he?"

"I'm pretty sure there would be no point in hiring me if that was his plan," Talon responded.

"I can't argue with that," Riordan replied. "So, we appear to have reached an impasse in our negotiations."

"It would appear so," Talon agreed.

"We tried," Riordan said.

"As required by court rule," Talon said for both of them, "even if minimally."

"Sufficiently," Riordan proposed. "So, this is just going to be a slow plea, huh? Have you seen the crime scene?"

A 'slow plea' is what overconfident prosecutors called jury trials they thought they couldn't lose. Talon was fine with letting him think that. Overconfident prosecutors tended to be underprepared prosecutors.

Accordingly, she let the first part of his comment slide by and answered only the second part. "Yes, I've seen the crime scene photos. Very... bloody."

Riordan clicked his tongue and shook his head in a way Talon was sure he thought was wise. "You know, when you're a prosecutor, you actually get called out to the murder scene that very night. Photos just don't do it justice. There's something about standing in the room where it happened. It always feels smaller than the photos show, like death is crushing in all around you."

Talon just nodded. She didn't mind him revealing his thought process to her.

He tapped the table sharply. "You know, I might just make a motion to take the jury out for a scene visit. Even after they clean it up, it's still worth going out and seeing the actual scene of the crime in person."

Talon nodded again and smiled.

Now there was an idea.

CHAPTER 9

Home sweet, blood-soaked home.

For some reason Talon had expected the crime scene to have been cleaned up. The bodies were definitely gone, removed that night by the techs from the medical examiner's office. The baseball bat was gone, too, secured away in a police evidence locker. But the blood and gore covering the walls, floors, and furniture had very much been left behind for others to clean. And after all that time, it wasn't just unsightly; it was rank.

"Oh, shit!" Karen Burgess exclaimed as she opened the door to her dead parents' home and was accosted by the sight and smell inside.

She turned away to retch, but her husband clicked his tongue and frowned at her. "Karen," he admonished. "Language."

"I—I'm sorry, Chad," Karen coughed after a moment. "I just didn't expect—" She peered through the crack of the door. "I don't think I can go in there. I just—I just can't."

Chad's expression softened and he put a hand on his wife's shoulder. "It's okay, honey. We understand. This has been hard for all of us."

Talon was pretty sure it had been the hardest for Karen,

since it was her parents who were murdered, but she wasn't about to get dragged into some grieving competition between her client's parents. She didn't care who had the hardest time, so long as one of them signed the checks.

"You can certainly wait out here," Talon told her. "I just need one of you to come inside in case I have questions about what I'm looking at."

"Of course," Chad answered for both of them. "Karen will wait outside. I'll go in with you."

Talon pushed the door all the way open. "Let me go in first," she directed. "I don't want you to inadvertently step on something important before I get the chance to see it."

Chad nodded. "Of course. Very smart."

Damn right it's smart, Talon thought. *That's why you hired me.*

But she didn't say that. She didn't say anything. She wasn't interested in small talk. If she had a question, she'd ask, and Chad better have the answer or Karen might be dragged into that house of horrors after all.

It was actually a lake house of horrors. The Burgesses owned a waterfront lot on Lake Tapps, about twenty miles east of Tacoma. There was a large, recently remodeled main house near the road where Chad, Karen, and Hunter lived. Karen's parents lived in the smaller, also recently remodeled home on the back of the property. They called it a 'lake house' but it was more like a full-sized rambler, over 1,500 square feet, with three bedrooms and one and a half baths. Not a bad place to retire. Until your grandson murders you, anyway.

The entry led directly into a front living room and dining nook. The kitchen was off to the left; to the right was the hallway to the bedrooms. There actually wasn't too much blood visible from the entryway. Just some smears on the walls leading to the bedrooms. And some dried pools of it on the floor by the front door. Probably where Hunter dropped the bat when confronted by the police. Talon stepped around the sticky black spots and made her way toward grandma and grandpa's room.

"We haven't been in h—" Chad started to say. But Talon stopped him.

"Shh." She put a finger to her lips. "If I have a question, I'll ask you."

"Right." Chad winked at her. "You're the boss."

Again, she both thought and did not say, *Damn right.*

Around the corner, there was more blood on the floor, and the smell of it rotting was stronger. The bedroom was a negative image of the hallway. The hallway had only a few small areas with blood. The bedroom had only a few small areas without it.

"Oh, shit," Chad exhaled.

Talon couldn't help herself. "Language," she chastened.

"Oh, right," Chad whispered. "Sorry about that."

Talon could have told him there was no actual need to apologize, but again, she wasn't really in the mood for extraneous conversation. Instead, she stepped forward to make a slow and careful circuit of the bedroom. She wasn't looking for anything specific. She'd already seen the crime scene photos, where the blood was still red and wet, rather than the dried blackish stains she was viewing in person. It was more about getting a feel for the space, to better understand how it happened, and maybe, just maybe, why.

But she knew there was no why. There could be no why that justified beating your grandparents to death with a baseball bat. Whatever Hunter's motivations were, they couldn't rise to the level of an actual why.

No why. No reason. Certainly no justification.

But the jury would want a why, Talon knew. They would

almost crave it.

She could use that.

She glanced around the room one last time. The cops had already documented what had happened, and what had happened didn't help her. She needed to suppress what had happened.

"I want to see the rest of the house," she announced. "Let's go."

Chad quickly acquiesced and stepped out of the room where his son murdered his in-laws. There were two more bedrooms to check out. The first one looked to be a combination craft and storage room. Someone was into scrapbooking. Probably grandma, but Talon didn't want to assume.

"So, it was just the two of them living here?" Talon asked from the doorway. She didn't see a reason to go inside. "No one else? Not your parents too or anything?"

"No, just Karen's parents," Chad confirmed. "My father passed away already, and my mother retired to Arizona."

They stepped to the final bedroom. There was a bed in it.

"Then why is there a bed in here?" Talon asked. "Guest room?"

"Yes," Chad answered. "And Hunter would use it when he stayed over."

"Hunter stayed over sometimes?" She liked that. "How often would he stay over?"

"Not often," Chad answered. "He lives with us in the main house. But sometimes."

"Not never?"

"Not never," Chad confirmed.

Talon nodded. "Good enough."

CHAPTER 10

Before she could file her motion to suppress all of the evidence they had against her client, Talon needed to confirm two things.

The same guard brought Hunter into the same jailhouse conference room where Talon had first met her client. They both looked about the same. Hunter might have even looked a little better. He must be enjoying the jail food.

"It's nice to see you again, Ms. Winter," he greeted as he took the seat opposite her. "I like getting visitors. You're my only visitor."

"Your parents don't visit?" That wasn't one of the things Talon needed to confirm, but she was a bit surprised. Then again, maybe not.

"Not yet," Hunter answered with a grin. "But maybe tomorrow."

Probably not, if they haven't come yet. Talon recalled Karen's reaction at the front door of her parents' home.

"Maybe," she offered. Then she moved to why she was there. Small talk with Chad was unhelpful. Small talk with Hunter was unsettling. "I need to confirm something with you."

"Okay."

"Where were you living when," she paused to choose her wording, "the night the police came?"

"With mom and dad," Hunter answered. "I have my own room."

Talon knew not to get into a discussion about why a grown man was still living with his parents. Probably the same reason his parents were paying her fees.

"And you lived there your whole life?"

"Not my whole life." Hunter shook his head. "We moved there when I was twelve."

"Okay. And when did your grandparents move into the other house on the property?"

"The lake house?"

"Sure," Talon conceded.

"I was sixteen," Hunter answered. "No, wait, seventeen. I think."

"Did you have a room there too?"

"Yes."

"Why?"

"Because sometimes I liked to stay there."

"Okay."

"Because sometimes I liked them."

Talon paused her questioning. Hunter filled the pause.

"But sometimes I didn't like them."

"Like the night the police came?" Talon knew.

"Yes," Hunter confirmed. His mouth was still in that same half-smile he always wore, but his eyes weren't smiling anymore. "Like the night the police came."

Talon nodded and stood up. "Okay, thanks, Hunter. I just needed to confirm that. I think we're done."

"Oh." His grin faded. "Will you visit again?"

"Of course." She knew she'd have to come back, whether she wanted to or not.

"That's good," Hunter said.

Talon wasn't so sure. But the visit has served its purposes. She had confirmed both things.

First, Hunter had had a room in his grandparents' house since he was a minor.

And second, there was no way in hell she could put him on the stand to testify to that.

But that was just as well. Mom was going to have to get used to testifying anyway.

CHAPTER 11

It took Talon a few days to draft the motion. She wanted to make sure she had the facts right. She already knew the law. She examined the police reports and confirmed the facts as the police reported them. She confirmed the police responded to a 911 hang-up call at the 'lake house'. She confirmed they went straight there and didn't stop at the main house first. She confirmed they never spoke with Karen or Chad or the dead grandparents before entering the home and finding Hunter standing in the hallway, blood dripping from his clothes and the bat. And she confirmed they didn't have a warrant.

Once the brief was finished, she printed out and signed the original to file with the court clerk, plus a working copy for the judge who would hear the motion, a copy for her file, and a copy to hand to Ronald Riordan, Chief of the Criminal Division.

But apparently, she didn't rate to see him in person.

"I'm sorry, ma'am," the young woman behind the Plexiglas in the lobby of the prosecutor's office said, unconvincingly, "but Mr. Riordan isn't available at the moment. He's very busy."

When Talon crossed her arms, frowned, and raised an eyebrow, the woman insisted, "He's always very busy."

Talon uncrossed her arms and sighed. She supposed that was probably true. Running what was essentially a law firm of 100 attorneys would undoubtedly require a lot of time. Although it was 100 prosecutors, so, in Talon's estimation anyway, they weren't like real attorneys. Not like her.

The court rules required she serve a copy of any pleadings on the opposing attorney, but they didn't give her the right to demand to do so face-to-face, no matter how much she might want to. She could, and apparently would have to, leave it at the front desk, stamping her own copy with the prosecutor's 'RECEIVED' stamp to prove service.

But it all worked out. Riordan called her not five minutes after she got back to her office.

"This is absurd," he began as soon as she answered.

"Nice to meet you, Absurd," she responded. "This is Talon."

"Don't be cute," Riordan barked. "I just read the motion you dropped off at my office. It's ridiculous."

"Not as ridiculous as thinking my client would plead guilty as charged to two counts of first-degree murder."

"They found him inside with a blood-covered baseball bat in his hand."

"My point exactly," Talon answered. "They found him inside. Without a warrant."

"You don't need a warrant to enter a murder scene," Riordan growled.

"Is that the rule?" Talon asked. "I didn't think that was the rule. I mean, I've read the Fourth Amendment a few times now, and Article One, Section Seven, of the Washington Constitution too. I don't recall anything about murder being an exception to the warrant requirement. 'Secure in their persons, houses, papers, and effects against unreasonable searches and seizure... unless it's a murder case.' Nope, I don't think that's in there."

"Exigent circumstances," Riordan shot back. "Community caretaking. Those are exceptions to the warrant requirement."

"Sounds like a legal argument," Talon replied. "We should have a hearing in front of a judge or something."

"Cute, Winter," Riordan sneered.

"I'm not being cute, *Ron*," Winter returned. "I will hold you to the law, and I will hold your cops to the law. And if the law says you fucked up and the evidence is suppressed, then that's on you."

"Your client is the murderer," Riordan said.

"We'll see," Talon replied. "We'll see."

CHAPTER 12

The hearing went perfectly. She still lost.

Talon arrived 20 minutes early. She didn't need 30 minutes, but she wasn't going to show up with only fifteen minutes or less before the judge took the bench. She was prepared for the arguments; she just needed enough time to make sure her witnesses honored the subpoenas she'd sent. She wasn't worried about Karen Burgess, but her other witness was on the other team. Sergeant Michael Unker of the Pierce County Sheriff's Department, the ranking officer to respond to the Burgess residence—residences— and therefore the one who made the call to go inside the house without a warrant. A reasonable decision at the time, Talon could concede, but the law wasn't always reasonable.

And cops didn't always honor subpoenas from defense attorneys. Another example of making a living off enforcing rules against others, while considering them optional for yourself.

Talon half-expected to have to start her hearing with a request for a material witness warrant for Unker's arrest, but she was deprived of the pleasure when she saw the uniformed deputy sitting outside the courtroom upon her arrival.

"Sergeant Unker?" she inquired as she approached.

"Yes, ma'am," he answered. He was in his 40s, thin but wiry, with a bald head and thick gray mustache. He seemed like he might be on the short side, but it was hard to tell when he was seated. Talon hadn't met him before, although it was certainly possible she had encountered his name in a police report somewhere prior to the Burgess case.

"I'm Talon Winter," she identified herself. "Thank you for coming this morning."

He held up the rolled-up paper clutched in his left hand. "Got a subpoena."

"That you did," Talon answered. "Did you happen to talk to Mr. Riordan about why you're here this morning?"

"Something about not getting a warrant before arresting your client, I believe."

"That's it exactly," she confirmed. "Any questions for me before we get started?"

"I don't think so, ma'am," Unker answered. "I did arrest him, and I did not get a warrant first."

Talon smiled and nodded. "Should be pretty simple then."

"The truth and nothing but the truth, ma'am," Unker replied. "I can do that."

"I'm glad to hear that," Talon said. "I have to go inside now, but I'll come get you when we're ready for your testimony."

"Yes, ma'am."

Talon smiled again as she pulled open the door to the courtroom. At least she didn't have to worry about Unker being cagey. That would make her job easier. She couldn't decide whether to admire his honesty about what he did or be horrified by his apparent lack of concern. She shrugged. It didn't matter, she supposed, as long as he told the truth. The lawyers would sort it out.

Inside the courtroom was the other of Talon's witnesses. Karen Burgess sat in the back row of the courtroom, her husband's arm draped over her shoulder. They both looked up when Talon entered. Karen's eyes were a little wider than they usually were.

"Miss Winter," she almost gasped. "I'm here. I'm ready to say whatever you need me to say."

Talon knew how that might sound to anyone who was listening, or when the Burgesses reported her to the Bar after she failed to get an acquittal for their son.

"I just need you to tell the truth," Talon was sure to say. "Simple."

Karen nodded. "Simple. I can do that. If you think that's what will help Hunter."

Talon considered for a moment. Overall, no, the truth was not Hunter's friend. That particular morning, however, viewed through the narrow lens of a particular legal issue sufficiently removed from who might have murdered who with a baseball bat, the truth had at least the chance of helping Hunter.

"The truth is always helpful," Talon answered. "Now, just sit tight until the judge comes out." She looked toward the front of the courtroom, and the side door where the jail guards would bring in their son, very much shackled. "When they bring in Hunter, don't say anything. You'll want to call out to him, but don't. It can only get him in trouble."

"Oh." Karen packed as much disappointment as possible into that single syllable.

But Chad was resolute. "We understand," he assured.

Talon extracted herself from her client's parents and moved to the defense counsel table at the front of the courtroom, just below the judge's bench. The judge wasn't out yet, but the bailiff and court reporter were in position, dutifully ignoring her entrance. Hunter would be marched in any moment. The only thing missing was the prosecutor. Or prosecutors, as it turned out.

The courtroom door opened again, slamming against the wall from being thrown open too hard, and in walked not just Ron Riordan, but also Cecilia Thompson, one of the best prosecutors in their office. And probably the only one Talon couldn't quite bring herself to hate.

She and Talon had tangled before. They were birds of a feather, if the bird was awesome lawyering and had blonde feathers on one side and black feathers on the other. Cecilia looked like the Swedish version of the Native American Talon. Or vice versa. It didn't really matter. What mattered was that Riordan was worried, which was good for Talon, but he'd added Cecilia to the case, which could only be bad.

"Talon," Cecilia greeted her as they arrived at the neighboring prosecutor's table.

"Cecilia," Talon returned the greeting. "I didn't expect to see you here. Your boss blinked."

"I asked to be added to the case," Cecilia asserted. "No one is blinking."

"I'm certainly not," Talon felt the need to say.

Cecilia grinned. "Good."

Riordan had been quiet up to that point. He looked over at Talon, but apparently decided to remain silent and looked away again.

Men, thought Talon with a roll of her eyes. *So emotional.*

But she could use that too.

The side door clanked open then, and in came her client, flanked by two burly and heavily armed jail guards. Hunter himself didn't appear particularly threatening, dressed again in red jail jammies with his hands cuffed to his belly chains, and his gait an awkward shuffle from the leg irons that connected his ankles a little too closely to allow for a full stride. He was also smiling, which under different circumstances might have been charming. Right there, right then, it was just inappropriate. She knew she had been right to subpoena Karen.

"Hello, Ms. Winter," Hunter said as the guards steered him to the defendant's chair and pushed him down into it. "Nice to see you again."

"Nice to see you again too, Hunter," she decided to say. She was under no obligation to speak the truth right then. She just needed her client calm and compliant.

"It's nice to get out of my cell," Hunter went on. "I don't mean to complain, though. It's a very nice cell. It's kind of small. In that way, it reminds me of my room at home."

Talon raised a palm at him. "Hunter."

His eyebrows shot up. "Yes?"

"Stop talking." She gestured over his shoulder at Cecilia and Riordan. "Those are the prosecutors. They can hear everything you're saying."

Hunter looked over at them and then back at Talon, his eyes narrowing. "Ah, yes." He grinned. "The enemy."

The judge took the bench then, bringing everyone to silence upon the bailiff's call of "All rise!"

There were so many cases and so many judges and so many courtrooms that it was not uncommon for a case to be heard by several different judges on its journey from arraignment to verdict, and so it was that Judge Holdbrook would not be presiding over Talon's motion to suppress. She was still stuck in the main criminal courtroom, conducting arraignments all afternoon, every afternoon, and accepting guilty pleas all morning, every morning. Instead, the motion had been assigned, essentially at random, to another judge.

Judge Gerald 'Jerry' Kozlowski. It actually said 'Jerry' on his name plate atop the judge's bench. Informality was something of a virtue in the Pacific Northwest, especially when judges had to run for reelection every four years. People liked voting for a judge named Jerry, the kind of name your buddy at the bar would have. It worked. 'Judge Jerry' had been on the bench almost twenty years and he'd never lost an election.

The good news was, he was as affable as the nickname suggested. The bad news was, part of that affability came from being a deep member of Tacoma's good ol' boy network. There was no way he was going to risk his friendships in the prosecutor's office, police department, or local media by suppressing all of the evidence in, and thereby effectively dismissing, a murder case. A double murder case. That had been on the news.

But sometimes, you just had to fight the fight, and tell yourself it was the good fight.

"Are the parties ready," Judge Kozlowski asked once he had settled into his seat above everyone, "on the matter of *The State of Washington versus Hunter Burgess?*"

"The State—" Riordan started, accustomed to always responding first, but Talon cut him off. It was her motion.

"The defense is ready," she interjected.

She allowed herself a sideways glance at the prosecution table, if only to observe Riordan's reaction. He was part of that same good ol' boy network. Pretty much every attorney in town who was over 50 and had a penis was a member of the club. He only provided her an annoyed frown, but Talon would take it. She'd get more later.

"The State is ready as well, Your Honor," he said. "Ronald Riordan and Cecilia Thompson on behalf of the State."

In her haste, Talon had forgotten to formally state her

appearance for the record. Oh well. They all knew who she was.

"I've read the briefing," Judge Kozlowski said. "I understand the claim and the response. Are we ready to call witnesses?"

That was judge-speak for, save your arguments for the end. Fine with Talon. She didn't need to do an opening statement for a suppression hearing. She was happy to get to it.

"The defense calls Michael Unker to the stand."

There were good reasons to call either witness first. It might make more sense to call Karen first to establish the living arrangements before then exploring, through Unker, how the cops ignored those arrangements, but Talon didn't want to give Riordan the chance to adjust Unker's testimony to fit whatever Karen Burgess said. Unker wouldn't need to hear that testimony to know to just answer 'Yes' to whatever Riordan suggested to him. That's why cops were called 'professional witnesses'.

Talon walked to the back of the courtroom, past the Burgesses, and opened the door to the hallway. Unker was waiting to be called, so all it took was a nod in his direction to get him out of his seat and headed into the courtroom.

Talon trailed behind as the sergeant stepped up to the judge, raised his right hand, and swore to tell the truth, the whole truth, and nothing but the truth. He then took the witness stand and Talon began her examination.

"Please state your name for the record."

"Michael Unker."

"How are you employed?"

"I'm a sergeant with the Pierce County Sheriff's Department."

"How long have you been a law enforcement officer with the Pierce County Sheriff's Department?"

Unker was clearly proud to answer. "It will be twenty years next spring."

Talon nodded. That was an admirable length of a career, even if it was as a cop.

"And how long have you been a sergeant?"

That took Unker a moment longer to answer, obviously doing the calculations in his head. "Almost twelve years now."

"What are your duties as a sergeant?" Talon asked. "As opposed to say a lieutenant or a detective?"

"Just like in the military, we say the sergeants work for a living," Unker chuckled. "Seriously though, my job is to be on patrol just like any other deputy, but when I'm on shift, I'm the first line supervisor. I respond to all serious calls, and I make the decision about when to bring in those other guys, the lieutenants and the detectives."

"All right then." Talon liked that answer. "Let me direct your attention to the incident involved in this case here today. Do you remember being called out to a residence on Lake Tapps that ultimately led to the arrest of my client, Hunter Burgess?"

Talon was careful not to identify any ownership or occupants of the residence in question. Unker didn't have any personal knowledge of that, but he would have assumptions. She needed to be careful not to let those assumptions leak into her questions, lest the judge hold her own words against her.

"Yes, ma'am," Unker answered. "I remember that call very clearly."

Talon supposed he would. She certainly remembered the crime scene, and it had been emptied of the bodies by the time she saw it.

"How did you come to be called out to that residence?"

"It initially came in as a 911 hang-up call," Unker explained.

"Trouble unknown. It was a landline, so we were able to trace the call to the physical address."

"Would you normally respond to a trouble unknown call?" Talon asked.

Unker shrugged. "It depends. Probably not normally, but if I was in the area and nothing else was happening right then, I might."

"Were you in the area?" Talon followed up. "Was anything else happening right then?"

"Not really, ma'am," Unker answered. "I was probably twenty minutes away, but it was a quiet night. I was going to let one of the other guys handle it, but I did start heading in that direction in case we got more information that maybe it was something more serious."

"Did you get any such information?"

Unker frowned. "Sort of. There was a second call to 911 from the same address where the caller hung up again. That time the dispatcher thought she heard screaming in the background before the line went dead. Based on that, I decided to go ahead and meet the other units at the address."

"Did you instruct the other deputies to wait for you?"

"No, ma'am," Unker answered, "because you never know what you're going to find when you get to a scene. But they knew I was on the way. I arrived just a few minutes after the first units."

"Did they in fact wait for you before doing anything?"

"They did, ma'am," Unker confirmed.

"And what did you find when you got to the scene?" Talon asked. "Was there any obvious criminal activity from outside the residence?"

She avoided asking about multiple residences on the property. She wanted Unker's ignorance of that fact to speak for itself.

"No, ma'am," Unker admitted. "It was quiet inside."

"So, did you just leave then?" Talon questioned, although she knew the answer.

"No, ma'am," Unker replied. "On a call like that, we're going to make sure everyone is okay before we just leave the scene."

"Do you do that on every 911 hang-up call?"

"No, ma'am," Unker admitted, "but we're going to do that if the dispatcher hears screaming in the background. Obviously, someone was in distress. I'm not clearing that scene until I know the distress has passed."

Obviously, Talon thought to herself.

"So, what did you do?" Talon asked. "Peek in the windows or something?"

"We did not do that, ma'am," Unker answered. "The shades were drawn, and the lights were off inside."

"So, you considered peeking in the windows," Talon restated his answer, "but it wouldn't have done any good."

"Correct, ma'am," Unker agreed.

"So, what did you do?"

"We knocked on the door," Unker answered.

"Knock and announce?" Talon clarified.

"Yes, ma'am," Unker confirmed. "We knocked and I personally called out, 'Pierce County Sheriff'."

"Did you do that from right in front of the door?" Talon asked. "Just exposed like that, or did you take up a more strategic position?"

"Initially, it was just in front of the door," Unker answered. "I mean, I stood to one side. I'm not stupid. But we were right there on the front porch, ma'am."

So, they didn't suspect any violence at that point, Talon thought.

She didn't ask that question though, lest Unker dispel the assertion. It was always better to argue to the judge what the witness really meant after the witness was off the stand and couldn't clarify anything.

"Was there any reply when you knocked and announced?" Talon asked.

Unker considered for a moment. "There wasn't a reply, but there was a reaction."

Talon tipped her head slightly. "What reaction?"

"We could hear someone moving around inside," Unker explained.

"What exactly did you hear," Talon asked, "that made you believe someone was inside?"

"It was like footsteps that suddenly stopped," Unker answered, "and a sort of scrape or thunk."

"A scrape or a thunk?" Talon repeated. "That doesn't sound very specific."

"No, ma'am, I suppose not," Unker admitted, "but if you'd heard it, you'd know what I'm talking about. There was definitely someone on the other side of that door."

"Did you think it was someone who had committed a crime?"

Talon hoped the answer would be 'yes', but she knew better than to hope for something when a cop was on the stand.

"It could have been that," Unker allowed, "but it also could have been someone who was the victim of a crime, or who was injured in some other way and in need of assistance."

Talon frowned at that very good answer. "So, what did you do next?"

"I made the decision to make entry into the residence," Unker said.

"You broke the door down," Talon translated.

"Yes, ma'am," Unker confirmed. "Well, actually we kicked it in. It didn't come off the hinges or anything."

"What did you see when you entered the home?"

Unker leaned over to look past Talon and pointed at Hunter seated at the defense table. "Him."

"You saw my client, Hunter Burgess, inside that residence," Talon wanted the record to be perfectly clear. "Is that correct?"

"That is correct, ma'am," Unker had no trouble agreeing.

"Did he appear to be in any distress?"

Unker grinned a bit at the question. "Uh, no, ma'am. He appeared to have inflicted distress on someone else."

Talon knew what was coming, so she went ahead and said it for him. "He was covered in blood and holding a blood-covered baseball bat, correct?"

Unker nodded. "That is very much correct, ma'am."

"Did you ask his permission to enter?"

Unker actually laughed a bit at the suggestion. "Um, no, ma'am. No, we did not."

"Did you stop to contact a judge to obtain a warrant to enter the home?"

Another incredulous chuckle. "No, ma'am. We were not about to do that."

"You just entered the home and seized my client at that point, correct?"

"Correct," Unker answered. "We immediately disarmed and took control of him."

"Handcuffed him?"

"Yes, ma'am."

"Removed him from the residence?"

"Yes."

"Then searched the residence and discovered the bodies of the victims?"

"Yes, ma'am."

"All without obtaining a warrant from a judge," Talon asked, "or permission from a resident."

"The residents were dead, ma'am," Unker replied.

"So says you, sergeant," Talon responded. Then she looked up to Judge Kozlowski. "No further questions for this witness, Your Honor. Thank you."

Talon returned to her seat and waited to see who would do the cross-examination. Riordan had brought Cecilia for a reason. Talon wondered if that reason was Unker.

Apparently not.

Riordan stood up and stepped out from behind the prosecution table.

"Good morning, Sergeant Unker," he began amicably.

"Good morning, Mr. Riordan," the sergeant returned.

Talon wondered if they'd both greet the judge and make it one big ol' boy reunion, but Riordan must have managed to resist the urge.

"How long have you been a law enforcement officer, did you say?" Riordan asked.

"Almost twenty years," Unker answered.

"Almost twenty years," Riordan repeated, nodding with admiration. "I bet you've seen a lot in those twenty years."

"Oh, yes, sir. I sure have."

"Every crime on the books, I imagine?"

"Yes, sir," Unker agreed. "And more times than I'd like to count."

"I don't blame you for that," Riordan chuckled. "You've seen the worst humanity has to offer. And every day at that, for twenty years now."

Unker frowned a bit and nodded himself. "Yes, sir."

"Why did you go into law enforcement in the first place, sergeant?"

"Why did I become a cop?" Unker clarified.

"Yes," Riordan confirmed.

Unker shrugged slightly. "I wanted to help people."

"You wanted to help people," Riordan repeated the answer again. "And over these last twenty years, have you helped a lot of people?"

Unker sat up a bit straighter. "I'd like to think so."

"I'm sure you have, sergeant," Riordan said. "I'm sure you have. Now, some of those people, they didn't need a lot of help, did they? Maybe they just lost something or needed directions? Nothing too serious, am I right?"

"That's correct, sir," Unker answered. "Sometimes people see my uniform and know that I can help them, even if it's just something simple."

"That's great," Riordan replied. "Just great. But, sometimes, it's more serious, isn't it?"

Unker frowned again. "Yes, sir."

"Sometimes it's very serious, isn't it?"

"As serious as it gets," Unker agreed.

"Violent assaults, sexual assaults," Riordan listed, "even murders, correct?"

Unker nodded. "Correct."

"And do you help those people too?"

"Of course."

"Of course." Riordan nodded along. "That's why you became a sheriff's deputy in the first place."

"Yes, sir."

"Can you help everyone?" Riordan asked. "Or is it too late sometimes?"

Unker thought for a moment. "Sometimes it's too late."

"But sometimes you get there just in the nick of time, right?" Riordan encouraged. "Sometimes the only person who could help them was you and the only chance you had was right there and right then, isn't that right?"

"That is right, sir," Unker agreed.

"Sometimes," Riordan continued, "the difference between life and death was your decision to help someone right there and right then, correct?"

"Very correct," Unker answered.

"And that's why you're a cop."

"Absolutely."

Riordan paused then. He was about to get into the facts of Hunter's case, Talon knew, but he also just wanted the attention of a dramatic pause. You don't get to run the entire criminal division if you aren't a good trial lawyer, and you aren't a good trial lawyer if you don't enjoy the showmanship of it all.

"The call-out on this case," Riordan continued, "it was a 911 hang-up call?"

"Yes, sir."

"Two, in fact? With screaming in the background?"

"Yes, sir."

"So, a potentially dangerous situation, correct?" Riordan fed him the answer.

"Absolutely."

"But when you arrived, there were no signs of an active dispute, correct?"

"Correct," Unker agreed, yet again.

"Which meant," Riordan suggested, "either there never was

a dispute, or the dispute was over, correct?"

Unker considered for a moment. "That's correct, sir. Just because it's quiet when we get there, doesn't mean nothing happened. In fact, sometimes it only gets quiet because we arrive, and if we leave without investigating, whatever was happening could start right back up again."

"So, there might be a victim inside who will still be in danger if you just leave?"

"Exactly," Unker answered. "Once we're dispatched to a scene, we can't just leave. We have to make sure everyone is okay."

"Because that's what cops do," Riordan commended.

"Yes, sir," Unker answered proudly.

Puke, thought Talon.

"In this case," Riordan continued, "you kicked in that door because you knew someone could be in danger and there was no time to waste, correct?"

"Correct, sir."

"How long would it have taken to get a judge to sign a warrant?" Riordan asked.

Unker shrugged. "Hours, maybe. Probably."

"Hours," Riordan repeated. "Did you have hours?"

"No, sir."

"And were you correct?" Riordan asked. "Was there someone inside who needed help?"

Unker considered how to answer. "They did need help," he sighed, "but we were too late."

Riordan paused again. It was a weighty moment. Or it would have been, if a jury had been there. A suppression motion, with just a judge? Not so much. Still, good practice, Talon supposed. And a good chance for her to observe him in action.

"And when you're too late," Riordan finally asked, "when

it's a murder and the victims are already dead, what can you do, sergeant? What's the one thing you can do to try to make things right?"

Unker knew the answer to that question. "We can catch the murderer, sir. And make sure he's held accountable."

"Did you catch the murderer, Sergeant Unker?"

"Yes, sir. We did."

Riordan pointed at Hunter. "Is that the murderer, Sergeant Unker?"

"Yes, sir, it is."

If it were the trial, Talon could object to a witness giving an opinion as to the guilt or innocence of the defendant. But it wasn't a trial. Judge Jerry would have overruled her. Besides, Riordan and Unker were on a roll. She hated to spoil it.

"And would you have caught him, Sergeant Unker, if you hadn't kicked in that door right there, right then?"

"No, sir," Unker answered. "I don't believe we would have."

"Then thank you, Sergeant Unker," Riordan flourished. "Thank you for making it possible to hold him responsible."

Riordan spun on his heel and returned to his spot at the prosecution table, where he declared, "No further questions, Your Honor."

Talon waited for the judge's invitation of, "Any redirect-examination, Ms. Winter?" then reapproached the witness.

"By the time you entered the home," she asked, "the victims were already dead, correct?"

Unker took a moment. Then nodded solemnly. "Yes, ma'am."

"Like, really dead, right?" Talon followed up. "Really, really dead."

"Um, they were dead, ma'am," Unker affirmed. "That's all I can really say."

"If my client had tried to flee the house," Talon asked her last question, "you would have stopped and arrested him, correct?"

"Absolutely, ma'am," Unker agreed. "He would not have been allowed to leave the scene."

Talon pointed at the sergeant. "Exactly."

She returned to her seat and confirmed, "No further questions, Your Honor."

Riordan passed on any re-cross, and Judge Kozlowski excused Sgt. Unker to return to patrol.

"The defense calls Karen Burgess," Talon announced.

She didn't have to go outside; Karen and Chad had been sitting in the courtroom watching the proceedings. Riordan probably should have made a motion to exclude her from hearing Unker's testimony, but he didn't, and Talon wasn't about to do his job for him. Talon had to turn around and motion for Karen to come forward because after calling out her name so dramatically, she just sat there, holding her husband's hand and staring sightlessly ahead.

Chad nudged her slightly and she stood up, almost robotically, then shuffled forward to where Talon stood—and her son sat.

"Hi, mom," Hunter whispered.

Talon slashed a sharp gesture in front of his face. "Quiet. Do not speak to the witnesses." She turned back to Karen and pointed to the judge's bench. "Go to the judge. He'll swear you in and then you take the witness stand."

Karen nodded, then looked down at her son, who was still looking up at her. Talon thought she was about to say something, but then she just swallowed hard and walked away to be sworn in. A few moments later, she was on the witness stand, eyes fixed on

Talon, who made a point of standing in front of her client.

"Please state your name for the record," Talon began.

It was a simple question, probably unnecessary even under the sometimes ridiculous rules of lawyers, but it served the dual purpose of introducing the witness and also calming her by allowing her to answer the easiest question that could be posed to anyone.

"Karen Burgess." The answer came in a quiet monotone.

"Where do you live, Ms. Burgess?"

Talon knew she needed to get right to the point. Karen wasn't going to last long on the stand, and there was no jury to impress. This was a rehearsal. Karen would get her starring role soon enough when they reconvened in front of a full jury box.

"21077 Lakefront Drive," Karen answered. "Lake Tapps, Washington, 98391."

Talon nodded along. She probably didn't need the zip code, but she wasn't about to interrupt.

"How many houses are on that property?"

Karen thought for a moment, realizing the question behind Talon's question. "Also 21079 Lakefront Drive."

"There are two houses on the property?" Talon clarified.

Karen nodded. "Yes."

"And you personally live at the 21077 house?"

"Yes," Karen answered after a moment.

"Could we call that the main house?" Talon didn't want to keep using numbers. It would get confusing. Words were better than numbers.

"Okay," Karen acquiesced.

"And the 21079 house," Talon continued, "is that a smaller house?"

"Yes," Karen answered. She wasn't giving Talon anything

beyond the bare minimum answers. Nerves could do that.

"Do you sometimes call it the 'lake house'?"

Riordan finally interjected. "Objection, Your Honor. Counsel is leading the witness."

That was true, Talon had to admit. But that didn't mean it was prohibited.

"Leading questions are generally prohibited under Evidence Rule 611(c)," she responded to the objection, "however, that rule gives the court the discretion to allow leading questions inasmuch as they may be necessary to develop the witness's testimony. Moreover, this is a suppression hearing and Evidence Rule 1101(c) specifically states that the evidence rules do not apply to hearings like this that are held under Evidence Rule 104 pertaining to preliminary questions as to the admissibility of evidence."

Judge Kozlowski didn't try to suppress his grin. "Very impressive recitation of the rules, Ms. Winter. A-plus on your evidence exam. Now, move along and stop leading your witness. I want to hear what she has to say, not what you have to say for her."

Talon nodded at the ruling, then turned back to Karen. "What do you usually call the house with the 21079 address?"

"The smaller one?" Karen confirmed.

Numbers were definitely confusing.

"Yes."

"I don't know," Karen shrugged. "Sometimes we would call it the lake house, I guess. It was closer to the water by a bit. I usually just called it mom and dad's house."

Talon had to grin at that. It was a better answer than what she would have fed her witness. Sometimes those rules could help a lawyer out after all.

"Mom and dad's house," Talon repeated. "Great. Now, are you married?"

Karen nodded. "Yes."

Talon jerked a thumb over her shoulder but didn't turn around lest she inadvertently give Karen a glimpse of her son. "Is that your husband seated in the gallery?"

Karen nodded again. "Yes."

"Does he live with you at the main house?"

"Well, yes."

"And your parents lived in the lake house?" Just to confirm.

"Yes."

"Okay." Talon took a moment. Mostly to make sure Karen was looking at her and not Hunter. "And your son, Hunter, did he live on that property as well?"

Karen frowned at the phrasing. "Yes," she almost asked. But Talon had been deliberate with her choice of words. Of course.

"Did he have a room in the main house with you and your husband?"

"Yes."

"And did he also have a room at the lake house?" Talon asked. "At your mom and dad's house?"

"A room?"

Talon resisted the urge to pinch the bridge of her nose. "Yes. Did he have a room there for the nights he stayed over at your mom and dad's?"

Karen took a moment to answer. Several moments. Too many moments. Finally, she blinked hard and gave Talon what she wanted. "Yes."

Whew. That was harder than it should have been, Talon thought. No way she was going to explore the nuances of those living arrangements. One more area of questioning, then she'd leave Karen to the assuredly untender mercies of the prosecutors.

"The night your parents died," Talon started, again choosing words carefully to avoid any implication of culpability by her client, "did the police ever come to your house or contact you or your husband in any way before going inside your parents' home?"

Karen thought for a moment. "I'm not sure."

Talon frowned. "Let me ask it a different way. The first time you talked to a police officer, was it to ask you for permission to go inside the lake house, or was it to tell you what they found inside?"

Karen understood that. "It was to tell us what they found inside."

"And for the record," Talon had to clarify, "what did they say they found inside?"

Karen's expression went limp. "My parents."

"Dead, correct?" Talon went ahead and led her again. Let Riordan object right at the moment.

"Yes." Karen answered, back to that low monotone. "They told me my parents were dead."

That was all Talon needed. "No further questions, Your Honor."

She returned to her seat next to Hunter. She expected to look back at Karen and see her finally taking advantage of being able to see her son, but her head was turned to the side, her eyes staring a hole in the wall.

"Cross-examination?" the judge invited the prosecution.

Talon expected Cecilia would do the cross, since Riordan had crossed Unker, but Riordan stood up again.

"No questions, Your Honor," he announced.

Talon's eyes narrowed a bit. She understood the instinct not to go after a grieving mother, but there was no jury to offend with an aggressive cross. And there were definitely some details of the living arrangements that could be clarified to show that Hunter didn't really 'reside' at the grandparents' house in the normal sense of that word.

But Talon wasn't going to complain. It was time to argue.

Judge Kozlowski excused Karen Burgess from the witness stand and she returned to her seat next to her husband.

"Any further witnesses, Ms. Winter?" the judge asked.

"No, Your Honor," Talon confirmed. "The defense rests."

The judge turned to the prosecutors. "Any witnesses for the State?"

"No, Your Honor," Riordan responded.

"All right then." Kozlowski seemed relieved the hearing was almost over. "I will hear arguments. Ms. Winter, this is your motion to suppress, so I will hear first from you."

"Thank you, Your Honor." Talon stood to address the judge but remained behind her table. "This is actually a very simple motion with an obvious ruling and a mandated remedy. The police entered my client's home without a warrant. That was an illegal, unconstitutional action. It violated my client's rights against unreasonable search and seizure under both the Fourth Amendment to the United States Constitution and Article One, Section Seven of the Washington State Constitution. There is only one remedy for such a violation, and it is mandated by all of the case law in this area. All evidence collected after the constitutional violation must be suppressed. In this case, that would include the bodies of the deceased, the autopsy examinations that followed from their discovery, and the documentation of the crime scene, including but not limited to photographs, diagrams, and video. It also includes the fact of locating my client inside the residence and any description of him then or afterward. In short, Your Honor, all of the evidence of the alleged crime collected by the State was tainted by the unlawful entry into the home and must therefore be suppressed."

It was a bold ask. She wasn't wrong to ask it, but it was still quite the demand. She'd need to go ahead and respond to what were certain to be Riordan's arguments. Or Cecilia's, if she were allowed to speak.

"The State will undoubtedly argue some exception to the warrant requirement," Talon continued. "They have to, because it is undisputed that Sergeant Unker and his deputies absolutely, positively did not have a warrant to enter my client's home."

It was probably less absolutely positive that the lake house was actually Hunter's home, but Riordan was the one who decided not to cross mom.

"But as we all know, warrant exceptions are not in the text of the Constitution. They are judicially crafted carve-outs from the general requirement of a warrant to enter someone's home. Accordingly, they should be applied sparingly, even reluctantly. And they do not apply in this case.

"The first exception I expect the State to argue is a sort of combination of exigent circumstances and community caretaking. There might have been someone who needed police assistance and there wasn't time to figure out what was going on or ask a judge's permission to enter. But this contention collapses under its own circular logic. They admit they didn't know what was happening, but claim it was that lack of knowledge that required them to violate the Constitution. If that were the rule, then the police could kick in anyone's door at any time, just in case there might be someone inside who needed help for some reason. That cannot be the rule and indeed it is not the rule."

Talon paused for a moment to try to read the room. Riordan was taking notes and ostensibly ignoring her. Cecilia was listening attentively. Hunter was too. But Judge Kozlowski had his arms crossed and a bemused smile on his lips. Nevertheless, she continued.

"The police need to have specific, articulable facts to justify their belief that a warrantless entry is absolutely required," Talon explained. "And if they choose to move forward without asking a judge to sign a warrant permitting entry, their actions do not escape judicial review. They may avoid it temporarily in the moment, but their decision to violate the Constitution is reviewable later, by a court, in exactly the hearing we are having here. This Court should look at the facts known to the officers when they arrived at the home, and it will be undeniable that they lacked sufficient facts to enter without permission.

"The only indication of any kind of trouble at all was a hang-up call to 911. When they arrived, everything was quiet. There were no sounds of a struggle or anything else which would suggest the call was anything but a wrong number. But despite the calm, almost idyllic scene of a small lake house on the shores of Lake Tapps, Sergeant Unker and his men kicked in the door, not because something was wrong, but because something possibly, potentially might have been wrong, maybe. It was a hunch, and there is no hunch exception to the warrant requirement."

Talon paused again to take a sip of water, then continued her argument. "As I said, the police decided not to take the time to seek permission from a judge to enter the home. It's worth noting at this point, that with modern technology and twenty-four hour on-call judges, getting a warrant is now a matter of minutes, not hours. But regardless of that, if the police didn't want to take the time to get a judge's permission to enter the home, they could have asked someone much closer and received that permission much faster. All they had to do was go to the main house and ask Karen and Chad Burgess if they could enter the home. A simple request, an almost certain agreement, and then the police would have had all the legal justification in the world to enter the home. Consent is another exception to the warrant requirement and Karen Burgess would have happily given consent to enter the home if she had any reason to believe her parents were in any sort of danger.

"But the police didn't do that either. They chose not to get a judge's permission to enter the house. They chose not to get Karen's Burgess's permission to enter the house. And having refused to ask for permission, they are now asking for forgiveness from this Court. But to forgive a constitutional violation is to violate that document all over again. Do not do that, Your Honor. Do not forgive their violation of our most basic and sacred legal documents. Acknowledge the violation. Label it. Do not excuse it. And then grant the required remedy. Suppress the evidence gathered illegally from that home. Thank you."

Talon sat down again and tipped her head just enough to see who at the prosecution side would stand up to deliver their argument. Part of her wanted it to be Cecilia, since it would probably be a bit humiliating for her to come to the hearing for literally no other reason than to carry Riordan's briefcase. But a bigger part of her wanted it to be Riordan because Cecilia would do a better job.

Riordan stood to address the Court, to really no one's surprise.

"Mr. Riordan?" the judge invited.

"Thank you, Your Honor," Riordan said, buttoning his suit coat. "I will make this brief. Generally speaking, a warrant is required to make entry into a private home. However, there are exceptions to the warrant requirement. Two of those exceptions are community caretaking and exigent circumstances. If either of those are present, law enforcement is under no obligation to seek out yet another exception in the form of consent by the homeowner. Here, police were dispatched to a 911 hang-up call with screaming in the background. When they arrived, the house was suspiciously quiet, suggesting that whoever had been heard screaming on the 911 was in need of aid. The officers were under no obligation to allow that person to languish while they spent hours tracking down a judge. Instead, the law is clear that they could enter, which they did, and when they did, they observed the defendant covered in the blood of his murder victims, the murder weapon still in his hands."

Riordan cleared his throat and glared disdainfully at the defense table. "This motion to suppress is, quite frankly, ridiculous, and I would apologize to the Court for having taken up its time addressing it, but that is not my apology to make. Instead, I urge the Court to do the obvious thing here. Do not suppress the evidence. Do not dismiss a double homicide case. Deny the motion and allow the case to proceed to trial where the defendant can be properly held responsible for his crimes. Thank you."

Judge Kozlowski nodded at Riordan as he unbuttoned his suit coat and sat down again. It was the judge's turn to talk.

"I am not going to characterize a suppression motion brought by the defense as ridiculous," Kozlowski began, "but neither will I suppress all of the evidence in a murder case—or any case for that matter—unless it is absolutely clear to me that suppression is required. In this case, it is not clear to me that suppression is required, because it is not clear to me that there was anything unlawful about the entry of Sergeant Unker and his deputies into the victims' home. Could they have done things differently? Could they have secured the house and waited for a warrant? Perhaps. But it's not my job to judge their actions in hindsight."

Actually, Talon thought, *that is exactly your job.*

"So, what I'm saying," Kozlowski continued, "is this: I don't find a clear violation of the warrant requirement such that the evidence in this case should be suppressed. The defendant's motion is denied."

Talon nodded to herself. She knew she shouldn't be surprised, but she couldn't help but be a little disappointed. She'd accomplished a few secondary goals, but it sure would have been nice to watch a judge actually hold the State to the law too.

"Bad result," she whispered to her client, "but it was worth a try."

"Yes, you're right," Hunter replied without looking at her. "That was a bad result."

The ruling having been delivered, Judge Kozlowski departed the bench to another call from the bailiff of, "All rise!"

The guards wasted no time packing up Hunter and hurrying him out the side door and back to the jail. Talon knew there was no chance of delaying a check-in with Hunter's parents.

"Not the ruling I wanted," she said when she reached their spot in the gallery, "but it was the ruling I was expecting."

"It sure would have been nice to have all of the evidence suppressed and the case dismissed," Chad replied, "but we didn't really expect it either, to be honest."

"Was it because of me?" Karen asked. "Should I have said something different?"

Talon shook her head. "It wasn't because of you. It was because it's a murder case, and no elected judge is going to throw out a murder case based on police misconduct. You don't get the endorsement of the police union if you hold them responsible for their mistakes. And you sure don't get the support of the prosecutor's office if you dump the case being prosecuted by the chief of the criminal division himself."

Karen looked down to the prosecution table. "He's the head

of the entire criminal division? They must really want to convict Hunter."

"He is," Talon confirmed. "And they do."

"Why?" Karen asked.

Talon wasn't sure how to answer that without pointing out the whole 'your son murdered your parents' thing.

Fortunately, Chad jumped in. "It's their job, honey. They're just doing their job. Now, let's let Miss Winter do hers. Thank you again for trying. You'll keep us updated on what comes next?"

Talon nodded. "I will. Thank you again for coming today."

Chad led his wife toward the exit as Talon returned to gather her things from the counsel table. Riordan and Cecilia had just finished packing up their own things.

"Excellent advocacy today, Ms. Thompson," Winter teased. "I can see why they added you to the case."

Riordan, at whom the comment was actually directed, ignored her. But Cecilia offered a smile.

"Don't worry, Talon. I'm still getting up to speed. You'll get your chance to see me in action."

Talon didn't doubt it. "May the best woman win."

CHAPTER 13

Losing always stung. It was the norm in criminal defense, and you built up callouses, but it still always stung a little. If it ever stopped stinging, it was time to find a new job. No client wants an attorney who doesn't mind losing. Especially if losing means the client spends the rest of his life in prison.

There was no avoiding the sting, but there could be breaks from it. Respites where the sting was momentarily forgotten. Even mirages of never feeling it again. And over a good cup of coffee, if at all possible.

The best cup of coffee in Tacoma was at an out of the way coffee shop called 'Midgaard', halfway between the downtown courthouse and juvenile hall, which, for some reason, the county leaders had decided to build on the other side of town from the entire rest of the court system. It was probably intentional, something about keeping wayward youth away from hardened adult criminals. It was also why Talon rarely took juvie cases. Still, the trip to Midgaard was always worth it, especially to flesh out the details of the mirage being peddled by Cassandra Sondheim of Erickson, Larson and Sondheim.

"Thanks for meeting me again," Cassandra said as she

glanced around the coffee shop. "Interesting place. I've never been here before."

Talon wasn't surprised. It wasn't high-end. It shared a one-story building with a tattoo parlor and the next-door neighbor was a vacant lot covered in gravel. The décor was mostly black paint with some weird original art, not all of it framed, hanging haphazardly on some, but not all of the walls. The coffee roasters and painted-shut windows made it both loud and stuffy. For Talon, the almost smothering atmosphere made it easier to forget her stings. For Cassandra, it seemed to inflict its own on her.

"It's an acquired taste," Talon offered.

The barista called out their orders, and in a few moments they were seated at the table farthest from the noise of the roasters and nearest the occasional breeze of fresh air offered by entry or exit of other customers.

"So, tell me more about this position you're offering me," Talon began. "I just lost a suppression motion I should have won and so I'm in a suggestable state."

That wasn't as true as it sounded—her callouses were pretty thick—but it wasn't entirely untrue either. She wanted to hear the best they had to offer so she could go ahead and reject it and get back to reality. She didn't need to be distracted by the siren song of the perfect job while she was trying to win the Hunter Burgess case.

"We'll pay you double." Cassandra came out swinging.

"Double?" Talon almost choked on her coffee. But she needed clarification. "Double what? I'm self-employed."

"Double whatever you earned last year," Cassandra answered. "Just show us your tax returns."

"Gross or net?" Talon asked. She could hope.

"Well, net obviously," Cassandra replied. "Not gross receipts."

Worth a shot. Talon nodded and took a sip of coffee. "Could we use my numbers from two years ago? Last year was a bit of a down year."

Cassandra chuckled. "I'm sure we can work something out. So, you're interested?"

"I'm interested in the money," Talon admitted. "Tell me again about the work. What would it actually mean to 'run the Tacoma office'? Sounds like a lot of staying in my office instead of going to court."

But Cassandra shook her head. "No. You'll be in court. Think of it as concertmaster instead of conductor."

Talon frowned slightly at the analogy. She didn't get to the symphony much. "Team captain instead of coach?" she suggested.

Cassandra grinned. "Sure. I guess. That sounds right."

"I don't even know what a concertmaster is," Talon admitted.

"It's the first chair of the first violin section and," Cassandra started to explain. "You know what? Never mind. The important thing is, you'll get to do as much or as little court as you want. That's kind of the point of running the place. It will be one hundred percent litigation, so there will be a lot of court."

Talon wasn't so sure about that. 'Litigation' was what the civil attorneys called lawsuits, but most of those cases never saw the inside of a courtroom. It was a lot of depositions and threatening letters until somebody blinked and a settlement was transferred from one account to another—with 33% to the lawyers, of course.

"What about the day-to-day?" Talon asked. "Personnel, payroll, vendors, taxes?"

Cassandra shook her head again. "There will be an office manager to handle all of that. A non-lawyer. You shouldn't be wasting your time on that. You're the lawyer. You're the talent. Let someone else do the boring stuff."

Talon found that almost as appealing as the money. She spent way too much time dealing with the day-to-day details of running a law practice. She wasn't just a lawyer; she was a small business owner. The idea of pushing the non-lawyer work onto a non-lawyer sounded amazing.

But she wasn't sold quite yet. They obviously really, really wanted her. And that made her suspicious.

"I'll need to think about it," she said. "Talk to some people. Get some advice. What's your timeline?"

Cassandra sighed at Talon's slow walk. "As soon as possible. We have some big cases in the pipeline, and we'd really like to get you on board as soon as possible. Can I make a suggestion?"

Talon was always open to suggestions. That's why she was having coffee with Cassandra at all. "Of course."

Cassandra leaned forward. "Look, there's a process, and the process takes time. I'm just the first person in the process. My job was to find you, communicate our interest, and determine if that interest was reciprocated. It seems like it is, or at least it might be. Rather than wait any longer while you consider your options, why don't we move the process forward while you do that? No pressure, no commitment, but no sitting around waiting either. Like I said, we've got some big cases coming down the pike, and we'd really like to have you in place sooner rather than later. The next step in the process is to meet the partner who's the head of our Seattle litigation team. He's a great guy and you two would be working closely together, especially at first as matters get transferred down to Tacoma. If things go well with that meeting, then the last step in the process is to meet the rest of the partners on the hiring team. Assuming they like you—and of course they'll like you; they're the ones who sent me—then we can go ahead and close this deal and get your name and photo up on our website. Sound like a plan?"

Talon was a bit disappointed to hear that Cassandra's offer wasn't quite an offer yet because she didn't actually have the authority to make the final offer. But Talon supposed it didn't hurt any to allow their process to move ahead. In fact, she would want to meet more people than just one person before seriously considering taking a job at a new firm. Also, double the money.

"Sounds like a plan," Talon agreed. "I'm pretty busy defending the accused and all that stuff, but shoot me an email, and I bet we can find a time to schedule those meetings."

CHAPTER 14

"Double the money," Talon repeated. "Can you believe that?"

"I'm not sure I can," Patty replied. "Do you even have a salary to double? I mean, how does that work? And what about benefits, insurance, retirement? I assume they have some sort of IRA, but do they match contributions, or what?"

Talon nodded along to her friend's questions. They were finally grabbing that dinner Patty had wanted to have. The timing was coincidentally good for Talon. She wasn't sure she normally would have sought Patty's counsel on the job offer—as a public defender, Patty was a government employee with full benefits and a pension—but if they were going to have dinner anyway, Talon certainly wouldn't mind hearing her thoughts on it.

"I'm not sure," Talon admitted.

"Well, you'll definitely want to figure that out," Patty advised. "I took the job at the public defender's mostly for the benefits. Jeff owns his own business, so the money is up and down, and private health insurance is crazy expensive. It seemed like a good idea at first, but I have to do all the kid stuff too, which was hard enough when Jack was little, but now he's in kindergarten and the teacher thinks he might have ADHD, and so I have to deal with that while Jeff is always working late, and—"

"Right, right," Talon interjected. "I get all that. But it's not even a solid offer yet. Apparently, I have to jump through some more hoops. Meet the head of their Seattle litigation department, then face some star chamber of hiring partners to see if I'm worthy."

Patty took a moment, then smiled weakly. "Of course. But, I mean, you don't seem like the kind of person to jump through other people's hoops," she observed.

"That's all we do," Talon countered. "Our clients get charged by the State and then we have to jump through all the hoops in the court system, also run by the State, just to try to get the system to hold the other side accountable for even one of the thousands of times they don't bother to jump through the hoops they're supposed to jump through."

Patty nodded. "I suppose that might be true."

"Just once," Talon half laughed, "just once it would be nice to win because I'm right instead of lose because of who I'm representing."

"I hear that." Patty pointed her fork at Talon. "Remember that case I mentioned? I just got the toxicology results back. They are not going to help my case, let me tell you."

"Sure." Talon shrugged. "So, like I said, maybe I'm ready for something besides tilting at windmills all day."

"Right." Patty simply nodded.

"I mean, some of the windmills are fun to tilt at," Talon admitted. "Figuring out how to convince twelve people it's maybe not even a windmill, you know? Even if your client told the cops it was definitely a windmill."

"Oh yeah, my guy totally confessed," Patty said. "Not sure what I'm going to do abou—"

"At least my guy was smart enough to shut up when the cops grabbed him," Talon added. "Although, I almost wish he'd given some explanation as to why he was covered in his grandparents' blood."

"It wouldn't have been a very good explanation," Patty ventured.

Talon nodded. "That's probably true. But I don't think I can put him on the stand. The jury will hate him. They will definitely think he was capable of what he's accused of. Still, they're going to wonder why he didn't deny it."

"Technically, they can't use his silence against him," Patty said what they both already knew. "The judge will instruct them about that."

"Yeah, because they're definitely going to do it." Talon shook her head. "Just like when they tell the jury the defendant is presumed innocent, even though every juror who walks in the door at the beginning of trial thinks innocent people don't get charged with crimes and wonders what my guy did to get himself into trouble."

Patty had to agree. "Yeah. And if you leave it hanging like that, no denial at the time of arrest, they'll just assume he confessed and you got it suppressed on a technicality or something."

"Too many court T.V. dramas," Talon complained. "They should do a series of innocent people getting wrongly prosecuted and a hero defense attorney uncovering the truth."

Patty took a moment then laughed. "Yeah, we don't actually do that. Not very often anyway."

Talon laughed too. "I guess not. But still, I can't let them just wonder why my client didn't tell the cops he didn't do it."

"You want them wondering about the State's case, not yours," Patty agreed. "You need someone else to tell them why he didn't deny it."

Talon put a hand to her chin. "Yeah. But it can't be mom or dad. That would be speculation, and the judge would never allow it."

"It's not speculation if an expert says it," Patty pointed out. "Then it's an admissible expert opinion."

"Yeah." Talon nodded. "That might work. That might just work. A psychologist to explain why he reacted the way he did."

"Exactly," Patty confirmed. "In fact, I might need to do something like that in my case."

"So, I just need to find an expert who will say that," Talon continued. "How hard can that be?"

Patty frowned. "Probably harder than you think. But if you find someone, let me know."

Talon didn't respond to Patty's request. She was already pulling out her cell phone and dialing Curt's number.

"Curt? Yeah, listen. No, listen. I need you to start some research for me. Yes, now. What? Why? Right now?" Talon growled to herself. "Fine. First thing tomorrow, then. My office. Right. Bye."

She hung up again and frowned as she put her phone away. Then she pulled it back out again and started tapping at the screen. Then she closed the screen again and set it on the table. Then she picked it up again. Patty just watched in silence.

"I'm sorry, Patty, but I have to go." Talon stood up. "I have to get on this right away, and Curt is tied up with some personal life bullshit or something, and I just can't relax and enjoy dinner if I have something like this in the back of my mind."

"Of course." Patty leaned back from her plate. "I understand."

"Thanks." Talon reached for her wallet but stopped. "Um, I don't have any cash on me. No one carries cash anymore, right?"

Patty waved an understanding hand. "I've got it. You get me next time, okay?"

"Great, great," Talon answered. "Sorry again. Say hi to Jeff for me."

Patty's forced smile faded slightly. "I would, but..." she started to say, but Talon was already gone.

CHAPTER 15

"We need a whore," Talon said to Curt as soon as he walked into her office the next morning. "A total whore."

Curt stopped for a moment, furrowed his brow, then nodded and took a seat across her desk. "I assume you're speaking metaphorically. If not, I'm open to it, but I think you and I should finally take a moment to clarify the boundaries of our relationship."

"We need someone with a Ph.D.," Talon spelled it out, "who will say what we need them to say."

"That's what I thought you meant," Curt responded. "But maybe we should have that other conversation, too?"

"No," Talon replied. "We are never having that conversation. We are having this conversation. I need a psychologist who will tell the jury that Hunter Burgess's complete lack of remorse or really any emotion is consistent with him being innocent of the crime."

"Is it, though?" Curt asked.

"Not the point," Talon answered. "I don't need the expert to say he is innocent specifically. I need him to say his reactions were consistent with innocence generally."

Curt thought for a moment. "They don't really seem like it."

"Which is exactly why I need someone to say they were," Talon reiterated. "The jurors will all think the same way you do. I need to give them a reason not to."

"I can be a very clear thinker," Curt defended.

"The last thing I want are clear thinkers," Talon laughed. "I want their thoughts to be muddied, confused, uncertain. A certain jury means they're convinced beyond a reasonable doubt. But a confused, uncertain jury can't convict."

"They could," Curt suggested.

"No, they can't," Talon insisted. "The judge will tell them they can't. The jury instructions say that in order to convict, they all have to be convinced beyond a reasonable doubt as to every element of the offense charged. If they have a reasonable doubt as to any element, they have a duty—a duty—to acquit. I need someone to help them have some doubt."

"You need a whore," Curt repeated, "with a Ph.D."

"Exactly," Talon confirmed. "Do you know one?"

Curt sighed. "I think I do."

CHAPTER 16

"Larry Jankles." Curt's proposed expert introduced himself to Talon two days later with an extended hand and eager grin. He was somewhere in his 50s, although probably not as far along them as he looked. He had a large belly, a bald top of his head with the hair on the sides in dire need of a trim, and large glasses with fingerprints clearly visible all over the lenses. Talon couldn't decide if his shirt was supposed to be off white or was just really old. His hand was sticky.

"Talon Winter." She resisted the urge to wipe her hand on her suit, lest the clothes get dirty too. She held her right hand out awkwardly as her left hand opened a desk drawer in search of an alcohol wipe. "Uh, thanks for meeting with us, Dr. Jankles."

"Call me Larry," Jankles insisted as he dropped himself in the guest chair next to Curt.

Talon found the wipe and tore it open. "But I can call you Dr. Jankles on the stand, right?" She wiped the sticky off her palm. "You do have a Ph.D.?"

"Oh, yes, yes, yes," Jankles assured with a wave of his hand. "Well, actually no. I have what's called a Psy.D. It's a new degree. Still a doctorate, just less, um, let's say 'stuffy'."

"Less rigorous?" Talon voiced her concern.

Jankles frowned. "It's very rigorous, thank you very much," he defended. "It's still five years and a dissertation. It's just not as, you know, theoretical as a regular Ph.D. It's more for practitioners than academics."

Talon frowned. She could spin that. She just wished she didn't have to. "I don't need to explain your doctorate to the jury, just so long as you have one. So, Dr. Lawrence Jankles is accurate, right?"

"Larry," Jankles corrected. "Not Lawrence."

"What does it say on your diploma?" Talon asked.

"Larry."

"Really?" Talon cocked her head. "What about your driver's license?"

"Larry."

"Birth certificate?" she tried.

Jankles smiled. "Okay, you got me. My momma named me Lawrence, but my daddy always called me Larry. And I hate the name Lawrence."

"Dr. Lawrence Jankles," Talon repeated. "Hate it all you want. When you're on the stand, your name is Dr. Lawrence Jankles."

"Speaking of me doing things for you," Jankles raised a probably sticky finger, "you know my rates, correct? It's hourly, plus a flat fee surcharge for trial testimony."

"Why a surcharge?" Talon inquired.

"You want me to wear a suit, don't ya?" Jankles asked. "Those things aren't cheap."

Talon frowned.

"I mean some of them are," Jankles allowed, "but I'd really like a nice new suit, you know? Like from one of those places where they actually measure you and stuff? Man, that would be awesome."

Talon closed her eyes for a moment and sighed. "Fine."

After all, it wasn't like she would be paying. Mom and Pop Burgess would be responsible for any expert fees.

"Oh, and one hundred percent up front," Jankles added. "Nonrefundable. Up front and nonrefundable."

Talon nodded. "Understood."

Jankles smiled broadly and slumped down a bit in his chair. "Great. That's great. So, what do you want me to say?"

Talon raised an eyebrow at him. He wasn't supposed to say it out loud.

"Um, heh, I mean," Jankles sat up again, "tell me your suspicions about your client and I will tell you whether there is a basis to support those suspicions."

Talon lowered her eyebrow again.

"Better?" Jankles asked.

He wasn't supposed to say that out loud either.

"My client is charged with murdering his grandparents," Talon started to explain.

"That case?!" Jankles shouted. "The one on the news?"

Talon sighed again. "Yes. The one on the news."

"I'm gonna be on T.V.?" Jankles grinned over at Curt and slapped him on the shoulder. "How about that, huh?" He looked back to Talon. "I'm definitely going to need that new suit."

"My client," Talon forged ahead, "is charged with murdering his grandparents. Specifically, he is accused of beating them to death with a baseball bat—"

"Yikes!" Jankles interjected again.

Talon took another moment to control her breathing, then pressed on. "He was discovered by the police still inside the home, holding the bat, and covered in blood."

"Wow," Jankles said. "That is not good for you."

"I know," Talon answered. "That's why you're here."

"Did he at least say he didn't do it?" Jankles asked. "He didn't confess, did he? I mean, if he confessed, you're kinda screwed, right? I'll still testify, you know. I still need a new suit. But yeah, I hope he didn't confess."

"He did not confess," Talon confirmed.

"Oh, that's good," Jankles exhaled.

"He didn't say anything," Talon explained.

"Really?" Jankles frowned. "That's weird. Nothing at all? Why wouldn't he say anything?"

"Well, see, that's kind of what we were hoping you could explain," Curt stepped in. Talon was busy pinching the bridge of her nose.

"Ohhh." Jankles nodded, way too many times, and raised a meaty finger to point at Curt. "I get it. Yeah, that makes sense. Now I get it. I totally get it."

"Do you?" Talon wondered aloud.

"Oh, yeah, definitely," Jankles assured her. "Like, why would he act the way he acted right then when we would expect him to act differently?"

"Yes," Talon confirmed. "That."

"If he hadn't killed his grandparents," Jankles added.

"Right," Talon agreed.

"But he did kill them, right?" Jankles asked.

"Irrelevant," Talon non-answered. "I just need you to say—I need the jury to understand," she corrected herself, "why an innocent man might not immediately protest his innocence and explain the circumstances he found himself in."

"Ok, yeah." Jankles put a hand to his chin. "That's a good

question."

"Perhaps it was the shock of the situation," Talon suggested.

"Sure, sure," Jankles agreed. "Like PTSD, but earlier. Like, not way after it happened."

"Okay," Talon was willing to go down that road.

Jankles frowned and looked up at the ceiling. "What do you call something that happens before something in the future?"

"The present?" Talon knew.

Jankles pointed at her. "Yes. The present. Exactly. Present Traumatic Stress Disorder."

"So," Talon realized, "still PTSD. I feel like that might be confusing."

Jankles frowned. "Hm. I suppose so. What about PPTSD? Pre-Post Traumatic Stress Disorder."

"No." Talon shook her head.

"Yeah, that sounds silly," Jankles agreed. "But something like that. Heck, there might already even be a recognized diagnosis for something like that. With a name and everything."

"That would be great," Talon encouraged. She shot a look at Curt. Curt looked away.

"Oh, and I should probably know if he has any history of mental illness," Jankles realized.

"Would it be a good thing?" Talon asked.

"I just don't want it to be a bad thing," Jankles answered. "Nothing contrary to what you want—er, what I'm going to find. I mean, I don't want to diagnose hyperactive schizoaffective disorder syndrome or something and then find out he was already seen by a shrink when he was a kid and they said it definitely wasn't hyperactive thyroid whatever I just said."

Talon considered for a moment. "That makes sense."

"Right?" Jankles almost seemed surprised by himself. "So

how about this? You find that out, and I will look into possible diagnoses. At my standard hourly rate, of course."

"Of course," Talon allowed with a sigh.

"Rounded up," Jankles ventured.

"Don't push it," Talon warned.

Jankles laughed nervously. "Yes. Of course not. But still, it will take some time to find the right diagnosis. Oh! And I should probably read the police reports, too."

"Probably," Talon agreed. "Curt will provide you with copies."

"Perfect, perfect," Jankles for some reason reached out to shake Curt's hand. "This is great."

Talon wasn't so sure.

Jankles let go of Curt's hand and stood up to shake Talon's again. "I'm really looking forward to working with you."

Talon couldn't manage to return the sentiment. But at least they had their expert.

Jankles thanked them both again and took a step toward the door. But then he stopped and extracted a slip of paper from his shirt pocket. "Do you guys validate parking?"

CHAPTER 17

The next step was meeting again with Karen and Chad Burgess. She needed to ask them if little Hunter had any history of the crazies. She also needed to inform them they would be paying the expert's fees, on top of her own. And she needed to take their temperature about the entire case generally.

The wheels of justice ground slowly, and emotions weren't designed to stay constant over time.

"Thanks for meeting with me again," Talon started the meeting. They were in the conference room again. Her office was just a little too crowded for what she wanted to accomplish. Physical spaces were important; they impacted people's moods and perceptions without them even realizing it. That was why courtrooms were full of wood paneling and flags. And that was why her conference room had modern furniture and a view of the water.

"Of course," Chad answered for both of them. "Whatever you need, whenever you need it."

That's what Talon liked to hear.

"It's not what I need," she said, "it's what Hunter needs. And what Hunter needs is a mental health expert to explain why he reacted the way he did when the police contacted him."

"How did he react?" Chad asked.

"It's more like how he didn't react," Talon explained. "He didn't thank God the police had arrived. He didn't take them to help his dying grandparents. He didn't deny doing it. And he wasn't not holding the murder weapon."

Chad nodded. "Okay, that does sound bad."

Karen didn't nod. She was just looking down and half frowning, as if her face didn't quite have the energy anymore to bother expressing her emotions.

"It will sound bad," Talon agreed, "if we don't explain it away. I can't do that. I'm a lawyer, Hunter's lawyer. They won't believe me. It needs to be a psychologist."

"Okay," Chad had no reason to disagree.

"And I've found a psychologist who will be able to explain why Hunter acted the way he did." Talon didn't express her personal opinion as to the value of the psychologist in question.

"Great." Chad was fully on board.

"But he doesn't work for free." Talon dropped the bomb. "And he isn't cheap."

Now Chad had a reason to disagree. But he didn't. "Well, that's understandable. No one works for free, right? This has already been a bit more expensive than we would have liked, but he's our boy. We'll do whatever we have to."

"I don't know, Chad." Karen finally spoke up. "This all feels so hopeless. Maybe... Maybe we should just the chips fall where they may. Maybe it's better to let him face the consequences of his actions."

Chad's face had no difficulty expressing his emotions. "Now, Karen. We talked about this. We're his parents, no matter what. Our number one priority is to protect him. Our job has always been to clear his path of whatever obstacles might lay in his way so he can maximize his personal actualization."

Talon managed, just barely, not to roll her eyes.

Karen managed to narrow hers at her husband. "It was *my* parents, Chad."

Talon was getting that temperature reading she wanted. But she didn't also want to watch the entire argument the Burgesses were definitely going to be having eventually, and sooner rather than later, it seemed. It was enough for Talon that she knew it was brewing.

"Anyway," she interjected, "the expert will need the money up front."

"You'll have it," Chad answered without looking at his wife. "Guaranteed."

"Great," Talon accepted the commitment. Karen looked ready to start that eventual argument right then after all, so Talon moved to the next topic. One also likely to cause strain between the Burgesses, and therefore perfect to distract from the issue of Dr. Jankles's fees. "There is one other thing. Is there any history of mental illness I should know about?"

Karen finally pulled off that frown. "Do you mean Hunter? Or us?"

"Sure," Talon answered. "Hunter. You. Chad. Anyone on either side of the family."

"No," Karen almost growled through her teeth.

Chad hesitated, then put his hand on his wife's. "What about your uncle?"

Karen pulled her hand away. "That was never diagnosed. It could have been anything."

"Is that something?" Chad asked.

"That," Talon smiled, "is perfect."

CHAPTER 18

Chad was good to his word, although Talon expected Karen may have had a few choice words for her husband before he cut the check for the expert fees. But a few days later, Talon had cleared the funds through her trust account, cut her own check to 'Dr. Lawrence Jankles, Psy.D.' (he needed to get used to it), and met the good doctor in the visitor's lobby of the Pierce County Jail. He was wearing a new, actually white shirt. Nice to know that up-front fee was being put to good use.

"Dr. Jankles," Talon greeted him. She made a point not to remove her hands from her pockets for a handshake.

"Call me Larry," he replied, extending his own hand for a moment before letting it drop again.

"Let's get used to Dr. Jankles," Talon suggested.

"Ugh." Jankles dropped his shoulders. "Lawrence Jankles?"

"Exactly."

And so that was how Talon signed them in with the guard behind the bulletproof glass at the reception desk. 'Talon Winter, Attorney' and 'Dr. Lawrence Jankles, Expert.' The visitor logs were public record. Worse, they were government records, so Riordan could, and undoubtedly would, examine them to see who had come to visit his high-profile double-murder defendant.

After signing in, Talon and Jankles only had to wait a few moments for the guard to buzz open the first of several secure doors on the way to the pod where Hunter Burgess was housed. They were led to a different meeting room from where Talon had met with Hunter previously, but it was essentially the same inside: painted cinderblock walls, lightweight plastic furniture, small. Too small for three people to meet comfortably. Apparently, that wasn't going to be a problem though.

"I think I should do this evaluation alone," Jankles suggested just before Hunter was brought in.

Talon narrowed her eyes. "What? Why?"

Jankles pursed his lips. "I'm going to make sure he understands what I expect to find, if you know what I mean. The less witnesses the better."

"Fewer," Talon corrected.

"What?" Jankles frowned at her.

"The fewer witnesses the better," Talon said. "Less milk, fewer cookies."

Jankles's face lit up. "Do we get cookies?"

Talon cocked her head at him. "Do the guards bring us cookies? Is that what you're asking?"

"Is that what you're saying?" Jankles still sounded hopeful.

Talon sighed through her nose. "There will be no cookies. As for the interview—"

She was interrupted by the opening of the meeting room door and the unnecessary announcement by the guard of, "Here's Burgess," as he pushed Hunter into the now crowded room.

Maybe it was a good idea to leave after all, Talon thought. It was already getting stuffy in the tiny cement room.

"Who's this?" Hunter pointed at Jankles.

"Larry." Jankles extended a likely sticky hand. "Nice to meet you."

Hunter stared at the hand for a moment with a troubled expression.

"Dr. Lawrence Jankles," Talon restated. "Dr. Jankles is a psychologist. I'd like you to talk to him for a little bit."

"Do you think I'm crazy?" Hunter asked Talon. "I'm not crazy."

"No one's saying you're crazy," Talon assured him. "But the jury might have some questions about what happened, and why, and what happened afterward. Juries always have questions. Dr. Jankles's job will be to answer those questions for them."

"Like why I killed my grandparents?" Hunter suggested.

Talon winced and shook her head. "No, not that question. I'm trying to avoid any questions quite like that. It's more of—"

"It's more a question of what the police did than what you did," Jankles interjected. "The jury might not understand why they did what they did, and why you then reacted however you reacted. That's why I'm here."

Talon was willing to go with that. "I'd always rather talk about what the cops did wrong than what my client is accused of doing wrong."

Hunter took a moment, then nodded. "Okay." He grinned. "I don't mind talking about what happened. I like thinking about it, but I never get to talk about it."

And you won't get to talk about it at trial either, Talon thought to herself. She was also thinking Jankles might have the right idea about her leaving. She wasn't really looking to hear Hunter recount the literal blow-by-blow. In fact, if her strategy worked, no one other than Jankles would ever hear exactly what happened that night.

"Great," she said. "Then I will leave you in the very capable hands of Dr. Jankles here. Doctor, let me know once you've had an opportunity to formulate your diagnosis."

"Diagnosis?" Hunter's eyebrows knitted together.

"Thoughts," Talon adjusted. "Let me know your thoughts." She jerked a thumb at the door. "I'm going to leave now."

And she did, to thanks and well-wishes from her client and expert. She flagged down a guard and made her way back out through those same secure doorways until she was in the jail lobby, and then outside once again in the fresh air.

Her day had ended earlier than she expected.

Just as well, she thought, unable to shake the invasive image of Hunter lifting a blood-soaked baseball bat over his undoubtedly smiling face. "I could use a drink."

CHAPTER 19

Downtown Tacoma had no shortage of bars and most of them were a short, and downhill, walk from the courthouse. There was a dive bar, a sports bar, the bar masquerading as a family spaghetti restaurant, the bar that had been there forever and everyone knew everyone, the cool bar where the defense attorneys hung out, the uptight bar where the prosecutors hung out (why would they ever need a drink at the end of a long day of no clients and no bills?), and that one bar that was always going out of business and coming back as a different bar.

Talon didn't want to go to any of those.

Talon wanted to go to a bar where she wouldn't run into any of the lawyers she knew. Lawyers went to sports bars. Lawyers went to spaghetti bars. Criminal defense lawyers definitely went to dive bars. So, what she needed was a place that wasn't a bar but still served drinks, and the part that wasn't a bar was a sufficient barrier to entry to ensure the average borderline alcoholic lawyer went to any one of those other bars that was closer and cheaper.

She needed The Cascade Steakhouse, on the main drag of Pacific Avenue but far enough from the courthouse to be outside the natural habitat of Tacoma's legal community. It was embedded in what passed for the financial sector of Seattle's little brother. That was probably why the dinner plates started at $35, and it was definitely why it was devoid of lawyers making their living off the misery of others, and always hoping for the phone to ring with yet more misery.

Talon wasn't about to spend $35+ for a 4 oz. filet, but they featured a small bar in the back corner—only four barstools—and an equally overpriced house recipe Old Fashioned that probably wasn't the best she'd ever had, but was in the top three. And no one there was going to ask her opinion on their latest loser of a case.

"What do you think of this place?" the man at the other end of the four-seat bar asked her. "I've never been here before, but my phone recommended it."

Talon was prepared to be annoyed at being distracted from her planned solitude, but Mr. Three-Stools-Away was distracting in his own way. A good way.

He was about her age, maybe a few years older. It was hard to tell anymore she was finding. He definitely wasn't the young and stupid type she would have been hit on by at that dive bar. He was fit, with a stylish fade haircut and well-tailored suit, the lavender silk tie loosened just the right amount to radiate both comfort and confidence. His eyes were ice and his jaw was granite.

"Smart phone," Talon replied. He looked good. But she knew she did too. She twisted her silky black hair over one shoulder. "Has it been here before?"

He laughed. "No, I'm afraid not. Neither of us get down to Tacoma much. We're more Seattle types."

Talon made a conscious decision not to let that ruin things. Yet. Seattle types tended to look down on Tacoma types. She'd give him enough rope to hang himself. "Slumming?"

The man didn't laugh at that. He seemed surprised, and a bit concerned. "Oh, no. Definitely not. I'm just super busy and never get away from the office much at all. I ended up down here on business today and decided to walk around and see what I thought of the place."

"And what do you think of it?" Talon asked over a sip from her Old Fashioned.

"I think it's great!" he answered. It seemed genuine, but Talon made a living out of seeming genuine. "Right on the water. You can practically touch Mount Rainier. Classic architecture. And now this place. And you. It couldn't be any better."

Talon appreciated the sentiment, or maybe how smoothly he delivered it. She picked up her drink and moved a stool closer. "I'm Talon."

The man smiled and shifted himself a bit closer to the bar, and her. "I'm James."

"So, you came to T-Town on business, huh?" Talon asked. "What kind of business?"

But James shook his head slightly. "I'd rather not talk about my work, if you don't mind. I came here to get away from work, not think about it even more."

Talon smiled and raised her glass. "Here's to that." They both took a drink and Talon noticed hers was already getting low. "Okay, not work. What else can we small talk about? Oh, I know. What do you do in your free time? That's classic small talk."

"What free time?" James chucked ruefully.

"That's kind of talking about work," Talon warned.

James nodded. "I guess you're right. Okay, I like to go hiking."

"Hiking?" Talon raised an eyebrow. "Everybody around here says they like to go hiking."

"Do you?"

"No fucking way." Talon finished her glass and set it on the bar top. "Let me guess, you go mountain biking too."

James grinned sheepishly. "Actually, I do."

"So, you're just a basic Seattle dude." Talon frowned. "Kinda boring."

James took a moment, then pulled out his phone. "Well, when I get to where I'm going, I do this."

He placed the phone on the bar between them and started flipping thru a gallery of nature sketches, mostly black and white, but a few with watercolor or something. Talon didn't really know. But they were really good.

"Okay, that's less boring," she allowed. "You did these? Are they paintings?"

"Um, no." James smiled. "I'm not bringing painting supplies on a five-mile hike or twenty-mile bike ride. But I can always bring a sketch pad, a pencil or two, and maybe a basic set of pastels. Then, if I want to do a painting later, I work off the sketch I did."

Talon nodded at the phone. "Do you have any of your paintings on there?"

"I do," James answered. He picked up the phone so Talon couldn't see the screen and started tapping and swiping. "Just want to make sure you don't see something you don't want to see."

Talon smiled. "Don't be too sure about what I don't want to see."

James acknowledged the comment with his own grin, but didn't reply directly. He set the phone down again and the screen was filled with a vibrant image of a river in a forest.

"Wow. Definitely not boring," she said. "Why don't you tell me more about that while I drink the whiskey you're going to buy me."

"Whiskey?" James asked.

"Yeah, and the good stuff too," Talon answered. "You can afford it."

James smiled. "I can."

Talon smiled back. "I know."

CHAPTER 20

Hunter Burgess wasn't the only one who was crazy. James left the bar early, missing out on what would almost certainly have been a lucky night for him. His loss.

They did exchange phone numbers, but just as things were starting to get comfortable enough to maybe seek out a new location, he suddenly froze up, said something about a big meeting in the morning, and left Talon to ponder what might have been. For at least thirty seconds. Then she ordered some steak bites and a water, and let her thoughts wander back to her case while she sobered up enough to drive home.

Everything was sort of on hold until she got the psych evaluation back from Jankles. Most experts could take weeks to get a report back to her, making sure every 'i' and 't' was not only dotted and crossed, but also peer-reviewed and double-blind taste-tested, or whatever. But good ol' Jankles wasn't the type to waste time with meaningless redundancies. He understood it wasn't how many scholarly articles backed up what he was saying; it just mattered that he said it. Which he did, in record time. Two mornings later, Talon opened her email to find Jankles's written report waiting for her. And it was exactly what she wanted.

In fact, she realized as she read through it, it was even more than she wanted. Not only would it be useful at trial, she could use it to take one more shot at getting the case dismissed before it ever got in front of a jury.

It was a long shot, but worth taking. The worst thing that could happen to Hunter Burgess was to put those facts in front of twelve people who cared about justice enough to actually show up for jury duty.

CHAPTER 21

It took Talon a little longer to draft the motion to dismiss than she would have liked. Then again, the truth was brief. It was the other thing that took a lot of words to explain.

She managed to finish it a few days later, shortly before the court would be closing for the day. She printed out all the different copies she would need and parked in a three-minute 'loading only' spot near the front door. She was unloading paper, and it would probably only take her three minutes. Plus, she knew she could beat the ticket.

First stop was the clerk's office, to file the original. Then the prosecutor's office to drop Riordan's copy off with not-Riordan. Then, if there was still time, she could drop the judge's working copy off at the court administrator's office. That last one didn't have to happen before 5:00, but the other two sure did. She hurried across the lobby toward the elevators, navigating the oncoming crowd of courthouse employees heading for the exits. Clerks and bailiffs, court reporters and legal assistants, prosecutors and defense attorneys. Including Patty Rodgers.

"Talon!" Patty called out over the crowd.

Talon winced but looked over to see Patty waving a few

people away. She smiled and nodded, but didn't break stride toward her goal. Patty tacked against the tide and charted an intercept course to the elevator bank.

"Talon!" Patty called out again as she reached her target. "I've been meaning to call you. I really want to get your opinion on my case. I'm just not sure where to go with it."

"Right," Talon acknowledged even as she pressed the 'UP' button. "And I want to do that."

"Great." Patty beamed. "Is now a good time?"

"Um, well, no, actually," Talon answered. She held up the copies of her motion. "I have to get this filed before the clerk's office closes." She checked the clock on the lobby wall. "In three minutes."

The elevator doors opened as Patty's shoulders fell. "Oh, well, maybe after?"

Talon shook her head. "I have to move my car. I'm maybe illegally parked right now."

"Oh." Patty frowned.

Talon felt bad. She did want to help Patty. It just seemed to always coincide with something else more pressing. Such was the life of a defense attorney. There were people whose lives were literally depending on them. She knew Patty understood.

"Look," Talon said, holding the elevator door open, "email me the police reports. Let me take a look at them. And then let's schedule something solid. That way, I won't be running around always doing something else. Sound good?"

Patty perked up again. "Sounds great."

"Great." Talon let go of the elevator door. "I'm looking forward to it. It'll be fun to figure out how to stick it to The Man. That's why we do this, right?"

"Right." Patty happily agreed. "Thanks, Talon," she shouted through the closing elevator doors. "You really are the best."

CHAPTER 22

Talon managed to get everything filed and dropped off before 5:00, and she didn't get a parking ticket. Then, to top off a successful mission, she got a text from James apologizing for his abrupt departure the other night and asking if she was free for dinner in the next few nights. She smiled at the text and absolutely did not reply for two days. Then she let him know, at noon, she was free that night at 6:00, if he was still interested.

He was.

But he didn't know any good restaurants in Tacoma. No worries, she let him know. She would pick the place and he would pay. He could afford it. He agreed.

There were a few options for high-end cuisine and atmosphere, so Talon decided to go with the one she hadn't been to in the longest time: 'Pacifica', a seafood and steakhouse on the hill south of downtown. It had panoramic views of downtown and the water. It was also surprisingly close to the county morgue. Talon supposed most people who weren't in her line of work didn't know about that last bit; it wasn't like the morgue had the same giant neon sign that Pacifica boasted over its entrance. Still, that bit of uncommon knowledge made her smile as she drove out of her condo parking garage and turned toward her dinner by the morgue.

She was at the last traffic light before the restaurant when her phone rang. She thought it was James and answered it without checking. She should have checked.

"This is Talon," she said, hands-free, of course, after a push of a button.

"Talon!" It was definitely not James, unless his voice had raised an octave or two. "It's Patty. Oh, thank God you answered!"

Talon didn't share Patty's sentiments about gratitude to the Creator. "Um. Yeah, sure. What's up? I'm just about to—"

"It's Jeff, Talon," Patty said. "He's gone."

"Gone?" Talon was pretty sure, but not 100% certain 'Jeff' was the name of Patty's husband and not her kid. Talon wasn't great with names, especially when she was maybe only ever half-listening when someone talked about their family.

"Yes," Patty confirmed. Then she seemed to choke back a sob. "I think... I think maybe he left me."

Fuck. The light turned green, but Talon knew she wouldn't be making it to the restaurant. "Left you?" she asked, even as she started the U-turn back toward downtown.

"I mean, I don't know," Patty answered. "I think so? Maybe? It's just been so difficult lately. And then I got home from work and there was a note, but it didn't say anything really."

"A note?" *For fuck's sake.* Talon craned her neck to see if she could another U-turn and head back to the restaurant after all.

"It just said, 'Jack is at my mother's'," Patty answered. "Nothing else."

"Maybe it's a work thing?" Talon suggested. "And he just wanted you to know where, uh, Jack is."

"No, I don't think that's it, Talon," Patty was trying to hold it together, which was only evident by her inability to quite do it.

"We've been—It's been rough lately. And then with my big case, I've been asking him to do more with Jack and I think maybe it was just too much for him."

Too much for him to help take care of his own kid? Talon thought to herself. "Um, okay. So, not to sound unsympathetic, but, I mean, what exactly can I do to help? I kind of have pla—"

"I'm not sure, Talon, but thank you for offering," Patty said. "I just—I just don't want to be alone right now, and I didn't know who to call, and I don't want to have to go pick up Jack by myself. His mother hates me; she always has. She's probably behind all this, I just know it."

Talon decided not to argue with whether you could know something that was only probable. Patty didn't need a grammarian just then. She needed a friend. She needed Talon, apparently.

"Are you sure this can't wait?" There was an opening in the traffic coming. She'd have one last chance to right her course for Pacifica. "Maybe he'll come back soon and if not, we could talk in the morning?"

The late morning, Talon hoped.

"Talon, please," Patty begged. "I don't know what to do. This is my entire life we're talking about."

Talon sighed. Then she let the gap in the traffic pass. "Text me your address."

"Oh, thank you, Talon," Patty almost squealed. "Thank you. You don't know how much this means to me."

I know how much it means to me, Talon thought with a frown.

She pulled over to wait for Patty's text, then sent one of her own to James. 'Raincheck?'

CHAPTER 23

The only way Talon's mission of mercy could have been worse was if, after receiving a passively-aggressive short response of 'Sure' from James, navigating her way to Patty's surprisingly difficult-to-find house, accompanying Patty to extract her son from her hateful mother-in-law, and returning to that same difficult-to-find house with an ADHD toddler whose grandmother had loaded him up with sugar, if after all that, Jeff came home and it was one big misunderstanding.

Which is exactly what happened nine minutes after they got back home and 30 seconds after Jack spilled apple juice all over Talon's very nice, very expensive, very much intended for James and not Jack, evening dress.

"Jeff!" Patty jumped up from the couch, completely ignoring the waterfall of apple juice running down Talon's leg. "You're home!"

"Yeah, sorry about that," he answered, closing the front door behind him. "Crazy night."

"I thought..." Patty started, her neck blotching red as she fought off tears. "I mean... I didn't know where you were."

"Didn't you get my note?" Jeff asked. He was just your

average everyday father and husband. A little under 6'0", dad bod, needed a haircut. His clothes were definitely not the kind to be worn on a hot date with anyone other than his wife. Unlike Talon's ruined ensemble.

"It didn't say where you were," Patty said. "Just that you left Jack with your mom. I didn't know if, um, I mean, when you were coming home."

"Patty." Jeff stepped over to where his wife stood frozen by the couch. "Are you alright?"

Upon arriving at the couch, he finally noticed his overdressed and juice-covered guest. "Oh. Hi. Sorry, I didn't know we had company. You are?"

Talon stood up and forced a smile designed to show she wasn't really smiling. "I'm leaving. Nice to meet you, Jeff. Jack, not so much. Patty, we'll talk later. I'm glad everything is okay after all."

"I ruined your evening, didn't I?" Patty asked.

Talon didn't argue with her. "We can talk later," she repeated. "Maybe now, you should talk with Jeff. I think that might do you both some good."

Jeff looked askance, first at Talon, then his wife. Talon didn't wait for their conversation to commence. She marched out the door and pulled out her phone.

'Nightcap?' she tried. But after several minutes, there was no response from James. And still no response as she drove home, parked, and made her way up to her condo. She'd missed her chance.

CHAPTER 24

Or not.

"Talon Winter," Cassandra Sondheim gestured to the tall, blue eyed, chiseled jaw man in the expensive suit walking into the restaurant with her a few days later, "I'd like you to meet Jim Stapleton, head of our Seattle litigation department."

"'Jim'?" Talon raised a bemused eyebrow. Then, "We've met."

Cassandra looked back and forth between Talon and 'Jim', her confusion unconcealed. "You have? Oh, I didn't realize. Of course, you used to do civil litigation with a real firm here in Tacoma, right? Did you have a case against each other or something back in the day?"

"I like to think my practice is also a real law firm," Talon extracted that portion of Cassandra's ramble to respond to. "A little too real sometimes. Hard to get your hands dirty from a forty-third story conference room."

"Hard to get your hands dirty if you don't show up," Jim responded.

"Or you leave early the first time around," Talon returned.

Cassandra's confusion only grew. "What are you two talking about? I feel like there's some sort of inside joke."

"No joke," Jim said.

"And definitely not inside anything," Talon added. "Your loss."

Jim's expression softened a bit. "You know, I bet we can move on and start fresh. Start over."

"Not likely," Talon answered, "if you're the Seattle litigation partner Cassandra was talking about. She wasn't entirely transparent about it, but it felt like that meant you would be my boss."

"More like colleague," Cassandra suggested.

"Colleague who owns part of the firm when I don't," Talon asked, "and who directs and reviews my work?"

Cassandra offered a nervous smile to Jim, whose own smile was shifting from bemused to almost smarmy. Definitely smarmy.

"Yes," he answered. "That kind of colleague."

Talon crossed her arms and clicked her tongue. "Yep. You missed your chance. No way it's happening now. Not least because you knew exactly who I was, and you didn't tell me who you were."

"How was I supposed to know who you were until now?" Jim protested.

"How many Talons do you know?" she returned.

Jim's innocent face melted back into that smarmy smile. "Good point," he conceded.

"So, we're done here?" Talon wasn't really asking.

But Cassandra took the opportunity to try to salvage her mission from whatever secret forces were ripping it apart before her very eyes.

"If there's some problem between you and Jim," she said, "from something that happened a long time ago—"

Not so long ago, Talon thought.

"—then we can make arrangements for someone else to help you get established down here," Cassandra offered. "Not everyone can work closely with everyone else, but that doesn't mean we can't make this work."

Talon's arms were still crossed. Her jaw was still set. Her eyes were still locked on Jim's still too fucking beautiful blue eyes. But Cassandra's voice suggested she had leverage. And an opportunity to see how valuable she really was to this firm and how they would handle a situation where a male partner had harassed a junior female employee.

"I'm not going to work with Jim here," Talon said. "Tell me that's not a deal breaker."

"It's not a deal breaker," Cassandra confirmed, almost before Talon got the entire sentence out of her mouth. She turned to Jim. "Thanks for coming, but it looks like it's going to be a girls' lunch."

Jim Stapleton took a moment to assess the situation, then pursed his lips and nodded. "Of course. Makes perfect sense. You two girls have fun. I'll check out that fancy place on Pacific. I've heard great things about it."

Don't let the door hit your ass on the way out, Talon thought. "Enjoy," she said instead, although her tone adequately communicated the unspoken thought.

Once said door closed behind said ass, Cassandra frowned desperately at Talon. "I'm really sorry about that. I'm not sure what it was about, but I'm really sorry."

"If you're not sure what it was about," Talon counseled, "then don't apologize for it. It wasn't about you."

"But I'm here to recruit you," Cassandra replied. "If it's about you and our firm, then it's about me."

Talon shook her head. "It wasn't about you. It wasn't about

CHAPTER 25

The best cure for an awkward meeting with duplicitous civil attorneys was a good criminal court fight. A metaphorical blood bath to wash away the lingering dirty feeling Talon had after spending too much time with civil attorneys who were trying to convince her to spend even more time with them. Perhaps a poor choice of metaphor given the literal blood bath documented in the crime scene photos, but it felt apt, so she went with it as she strode into the courtroom the next week to try, against all odds, to convince an elected judge to throw out a shockingly violent double murder case.

There was a mental trick criminal defense attorneys played on themselves. It wasn't voluntary as much as they couldn't keep doing the job if their brain didn't do it. No matter how hopeless the case or motion, no matter how stacked against them the law and the facts were, the best defense attorneys—the ones who were going to make a career out of it without burning out and caving in on every case—were able to suspend disbelief and somehow convince themselves they might actually win. Not just might win, but should win.

And so it was that morning, as Talon strode forward to take

her place at the defense table, ready for battle. Ready for victory.

Of course, the other side would have something to say about that. Especially if the other side finally let Cecilia Thompson do the saying.

"This is a completely ridiculous motion," Cecilia greeted her. "You know that, right?"

"I know the State failed to preserve exculpatory evidence," Talon replied, "thereby depriving my client of due process, prepared counsel, and a fair trial under the Fifth, Sixth, and Fourteenth Amendments to the United States Constitution."

Cecilia sighed. "Really? We're going to do this?"

"I am," Talon assured. "You should feel free to concede."

Cecilia's only response was an eye roll before the guards brought Hunter into the courtroom and Talon turned her attention to her client.

"Hello, Ms. Winter," Hunter said as the guards shoved him into the chair next to her. "Always good to see you. We have another motion, I take it? Are we going to win this time, perhaps?"

It was one thing to delude yourself into thinking you might just win. It was another thing to make promises. "I hope so. And I'll do everything I can to. And if not, we'll get ready to win at trial."

Hunter nodded. "That's what I thought you would say."

Talon's bubble, if not burst, at least started to wobble a bit. The perfect time for the judge to take the bench.

"All rise!" called out the bailiff, before heralding the judge by name and rank.

They'd drawn Kozlowski again. And after presiding over two substantive pretrial motions, it was a good bet the case would stay with him for trial, too. Talon knew she could have done worse. She also knew there wasn't anything she could do about the assignment anyway.

"Please be seated," Judge Kozlowski instructed as he, too, sat down, albeit above everyone else. "Are the parties ready on the matter of *The State of Washington versus Hunter Burgess*?"

Again, it was Talon's motion, but again, the prosecutors felt entitled to speak first.

"The State is ready," Cecilia announced. Riordan remained seated, his chin resting on his hand. He didn't look at Talon when she glanced his way. He seemed annoyed to even be there if he wasn't going to be the one doing the talking.

"The defense is ready as well, Your Honor," Talon confirmed.

"All right then." Kozlowski nodded. "Good. So, is there going to be any testimony, or is this legal argument only? I didn't see any witness lists filed for this hearing."

"No witnesses, Your Honor," Talon answered. "At least not from the defense. It's purely a legal argument."

"No witnesses from the State either, Your Honor," Cecilia responded, "although we disagree that it's purely legal. We will be taking issue with the failure of the defense to call any witnesses."

Kozlowski smiled. "So, a legal argument, conditioned on a preliminary legal argument. This is what happens when you put a bunch of lawyers in a room, I guess."

Talon didn't respond to that. It didn't really call for a response, and anything she did say would likely rub the judge the wrong way anyway. Not what you wanted to do right before a big hearing.

"I will hear first from Ms. Winter." Judge Kozlowski nodded down to her. "Whenever you're ready, counsel. I'm looking forward to hearing your argument."

On the surface, that might have seemed like a good thing: the judge showing interest in the defense's motion. Talon knew better. It signaled a definite amount of incredulity. The judicial version of 'This oughta be good.'

"Thank you, Your Honor," Talon said anyway. "This is a motion to dismiss for government misconduct, and specifically the knowing failure to preserve evidence which would have cast doubt on the legal culpability of my client. There is no way to reconstruct this evidence and the defendant is now left unable to present what could have been the single most effective defense to the charges against him. Specifically, Your Honor, I am talking about the failure of the police and prosecution to conduct any sort of mental health assessment or examination of Mr. Burgess in the hours immediately after the incident which gave rise to the charges."

Judge Kozlowski was resting his chin on his hand but managed to raise an eyebrow at Talon's introduction. At least he was listening.

"The allegations in this case are, if I'm candid, shocking," Talon admitted. "We've all been doing this for a while now. We've all seen plenty of murder cases, and I think we would all agree that most of them involve some combination of anger, alcohol or drugs, and a weapon. Someone under the influence gets angry and makes a split-second decision to take another person's life. Often, it's a single gunshot or a single knife stab or even a single punch coupled with a skull bouncing off the sidewalk at exactly the wrong angle. In those cases, we can understand the motivations, even if we tell ourselves we would never quite do what the defendant in those cases did.

"But here, in this case, what the police found in that bedroom was nothing short of crazy. There is no way the police officers who saw that scene wouldn't have at least suspected there may have been a mental illness involved. And there is even less of a chance that the prosecutors who reviewed the initial reports and crime scene photos wouldn't have known that mental conditions like diminished capacity or insanity might have been at play. Mental conditions which would be complete defenses to the charges, even the charge of murder."

Talon was correct. Diminished capacity meant a defendant was suffering from a mental disease or defect that prevented him from forming the intent to commit the crime. Insanity meant he intended it, but he didn't know it was wrong. If either of those things existed at the time of the offense, he could not be convicted.

Of course, it was hard to beat two people to death accidentally. And it was even harder to believe you wouldn't know it was wrong, especially when you lawyered up when the cops caught you literally red-handed. But there was an old saying among old lawyers: when the facts are against you, pound on the law.

There was another old saying among old criminal defense lawyers: always pound on the cops and the prosecutors. Accusing them of misconduct distracted from what your client allegedly, probably, definitely did. Talon had lost the last motion because the facts were against her, she told herself. So, this motion she was going to focus on the law. The only facts she needed were the undeniable fact that the State made no effort to assess Hunter's mental state, and the fact that Hunter's mental state was anything but normal.

It was that second fact that Cecilia was going to go after, Talon knew. In part because Cecilia couldn't really deny the first one. Talon also knew it was the genesis of Cecilia's complaint that Talon wouldn't be calling any witnesses. But there was no way she was going to give the prosecution more than one shot at cross-examining Doc Jankles.

"By failing to even attempt to assess my client's mental condition in the immediate aftermath of the event," Talon continued, "the State allowed that vital and exculpatory evidence to slip away. And they did so knowing full well what they were doing." She pointed toward the prosecution table. "They may well argue that my client could still be evaluated now, and indeed recently has been, and that the expert can still give his opinion about what he thinks might have been going on at the time of the offense, but I guarantee you, Your Honor, one of their lines of attack at trial will be that our expert's evaluation occurred so long after the incident that it can't be reliable. That's what they always argue. And they knew that too when they decided to ignore, nay, cover up, what was happening with my client's mental abilities in the minutes and hours during and immediately after one of the most gruesome, unexplainable, insane murders any of us has had the professional displeasure to be associated with."

Talon took a moment to read the room, albeit through the quickest of stolen glances. Riordan's chin was still on his fist, trying to look bored. Cecilia was sitting up straight, a combination of eager and—dare Talon hope?—concerned. And Judge Kozlowski seemed... interested? She could hope.

"The remedy for failure to preserve exculpatory evidence is well established, Your Honor," Talon continued. "It is rooted in the undeniable fact that the system has all of the power, and the individual defendant has none. Indeed, any ability to act was forcibly taken from Mr. Burgess when he was arrested by the police. I had not yet been retained and therefore could not have done anything to preserve the evidence that is now forever lost. The police control the scene. The prosecution controls what happens next. They both knew this one was different. They both knew there was something wrong. And they both knew if they did assess Mr. Burgess's mental condition, the results could only help him. That's precisely why they didn't do it. And that's also why this Court must dismiss this case. Thank you."

As Talon sat down, Hunter leaned over to her. "I'm not crazy."

"This isn't about you," Talon whispered back. "It's about them."

"Still," Hunter frowned, "I don't appreciate the insinuation."

"Noted," Talon responded. "Now be quiet so I can hear their response."

Their response was to be delivered by Cecilia. Talon agreed with that decision. Riordan would bluster about how ridiculous Talon's argument was without actually responding to its merits. Cecilia would be able to communicate a similar level of disdain while actually rebutting the legal argument point by point. Or try to, anyway.

"May it please the Court, Cecilia Thompson appearing on behalf of the State of Washington," she began formally. "I'd like to begin by congratulating Ms. Winter on crafting an original and creative motion to dismiss a case of the most serious charges that can be brought against a criminal defendant. Indeed, it is so original and creative that I don't believe anyone else ever has or would have the, let's call it confidence, to bring such a motion."

Talon was watching Cecilia intently. She was a bit surprised by the personal nature of her opening attack. But she wasn't upset by it. It suggested a lack of, let's call it confidence, in her actual legal argument.

"There is ample case law," Cecilia continued, "addressing what a court should do when evidence is lost in a case, whether intentionally as the defense usually claims, or inadvertently, as is usually the actual case. That case law draws a significant and important decision between two types of evidence: evidence that is actually exculpatory and evidence which merely had the potential to perhaps be exculpatory. There is little to no case law about the situation where the State loses inculpatory evidence. Defendants rarely complain about that. But defendants regularly seek to conflate potentially exculpatory evidence with actually exculpatory evidence, and to elevate their claim of potentiality to one of certainty."

She's not wrong, Talon knew.

"The reason for this disingenuity," Cecilia flashed the quickest of glances at Talon, "is because of the difference in remedies. In the situation where everyone agrees the evidence in question was truly exculpatory—that it really did cast doubt on the defendant's guilt or even affirmatively supported the defendant's innocence—then destruction of that evidence and the resultant inability of the jury to consider it would undeniably impact a defendant's right to a fair trial. But this almost never happens, and certainly it should never happen. Police collect evidence and prosecutors file charges in an effort to reveal truth, not conceal it."

Wow, think highly of yourself much? Talon suppressed an eye roll.

"And for the very few times when an individual police officer or individual prosecutor violates this basic tenet, this sacred trust," Cecilia conceded, "then dismissal is often the only fair and just remedy."

She paused again to look fully at the defense table, and specifically at Hunter Burgess.

"But that is not the case here, Your Honor," she said, turning her attention back to the bench. "In this case, the evidence Ms. Winter claims was not preserved is speculative at best, and non-existent at its most likely. The State must preserve evidence it finds, but it is under no obligation to seek out additional evidence that may be helpful to a defendant. That is the job of the defense attorney, and while Ms. Winter may not have been at the crime scene at the same time as the first responders, she was retained quickly enough to appear at the arraignment the next day. If she truly felt, as she claims here today, that her client's mental state that close to the murders was so vital, she could have and indeed would have had her client undergo a mental health examination immediately, rather than waiting weeks and months to allow it to fester into an issue upon which to hang yet another quixotic pretrial motion, hoping a judge will do what she knows a jury never will, namely allow her client to escape responsibility for the almost indescribably brutal murders of his own grandparents as they lay sleeping and helpless in their beds."

"They weren't asleep," Hunter leaned over to whisper in Talon's ear. "I mean, not after it started anyway."

"Shh!" Talon hissed at him, for more than one reason.

"To the extent there may have been any evidence lost in the hours and days following the murders," Cecilia argued, "the blame for that falls at least equally on Ms. Winter. And the remedy for the defense attorney failing to gather potentially exculpatory evidence is most certainly not dismissal of the State's charges.

"The Court should see Ms. Winter's argument for what it is, little more than theater to placate a difficult client, and deny her motion to dismiss. The State is ready to present this case to a jury, Your Honor, and Ms. Winter should prepare herself as well. Thank you."

It was definitely a more personal attack than Talon had expected. But Riordan gave his assistant a pat on the back as she sat down. Kozlowski wasn't Cecilia's only audience. Talon found that disappointing.

"This is your motion, Ms. Winter," Judge Kozlowski nodded down at her, "so you get the last word. Any reply?"

Talon stood up. "Yes, Your Honor." *Of course.* "It may have been difficult to notice among the personal attacks against me, but Ms. Thompson failed almost entirely to address any of the points I raised in my motion. Instead, she engages in burden-shifting and claims I should have done her job for her. She forgets, for now anyway, that she represents the State and the people—all the people, including Mr. Burgess. I'm sure she'll remember that again when she reclaims that moral high ground with the jury, as prosecutors are wont to do. But here, today, the State is trying to avoid its responsibility to ensure that my client, like every criminal defendant, receives a fair trial. I wish I were surprised. In fact, in all candor, I am a bit surprised. And more than a little disappointed. But that's their choice. Your Honor has his own choice now: hold the State accountable for their failure to preserve exculpatory evidence and safeguard my client's right to a fair trial, or look the other way, blinded to the State's misdeeds by the glare of the accusations against my client. I can only urge the Court to choose to protect my client, protect the Constitution, protect our fundamental notions of due process and fair play, and grant my motion to dismiss for the undeniable, unremediable, and unforgiveable governmental misconduct in this case. Thank you."

That deluded state of actually thinking she would win a motion everyone else knew she had to lose began to fade as Talon sat down again. The arguments were over, so she didn't need it anymore, and her mind reacted by returning, albeit slowly, to a more sustainable state of reality and rationalization. That was a defense mechanism too. It made it easier to hear the ruling from the bench.

"I guess I'd like to start by thanking both counsel for their passionate arguments," Judge Kozlowski began, "and by instructing the both of you to dispense with the personal attacks in future arguments. We all have a job to do here, and the system only works if we all do our best. I never want to hear a lawyer being disparaged for doing their job, but I take great exception to it when the person casting the aspersions is a lawyer themself. I tolerated it here today, but I will not tolerate it any further. Do your jobs and make your arguments, but my courtroom is no place for accusations of personal misconduct."

He didn't ask if they understood. They did.

"That being said," he continued, "my courtroom is exactly the place for accusations of professional misconduct, especially accusations against the government brought by a criminal defendant. This is exactly the place for that, and I appreciate that both sides feel strongly about the merits of this present motion. I do as well. Each of you are charged with representing your side to the best of your ability. I am charged with protecting justice. I am responsible not only to ensure that both sides get an opportunity to present their cases to the Court and the jury, but I am also charged with safeguarding the rights of the accused, including his rights to due process and a fair trial."

Talon liked where Kozlowski was going. So far, anyway.

"An accusation of government misconduct which actually affects a defendant's right to a fair trial is extremely serious," the judge went on. "It might be the most serious charge a defendant can make against the State. But it is also one that is routinely made by defendants, whether or not it's supported by the law and the facts. Indeed, this is the second time on this case alone I have presided over an accusation of misconduct by state actors, and I won't be surprised if it's not the last time."

Talon liked that direction less.

"Ms. Winter is correct. Failure to preserve exculpatory evidence is a serious matter and, when proved, results in dismissal of the charges. This is because the State has made it impossible for the defendant to receive a fair trial. But Ms. Thompson is right that the Court must first make the threshold determination of whether the evidence was in fact exculpatory, and only then decide whether its loss was due to government action. I would add to that a second threshold determination of whether the evidence was indeed lost."

Talon hated that direction.

"Defendants face a catch-22 in motions like this," Judge Kozlowski conceded. "The State always argues that the defendant hasn't shown the evidence was truly exculpatory, but how can the defendant do that if it's been destroyed? And so, I think the better question, or at least one that we can use here to avoid that problem, is whether the evidence was actually lost. And I think, in this case, it probably has not been."

Crap.

"Ms. Winter attached, in support of her motion, a forensic psychological report from Dr. Lawrence Jankles. Dr. Jankles made several conclusions regarding Mr. Burgess's mental state at the time of his arrest, and so to that extent, it appears the evidence Ms. Winter claims has been lost can actually be presented to the jury after all."

"Thank you, Your Honor," Cecilia interjected.

"Don't thank me yet, Ms. Thompson," Judge Kozlowski warned her. "Ms. Winter made an excellent point when she predicted you and Mr. Riordan would certainly attack Dr. Jankles's opinion based in part on the gap in time between the event and the evaluation. And if you are allowed to do that, I think that bolsters Ms. Winter's claim that an evaluation immediately after the incident is different in kind from a later evaluation. And if that's true, then that earlier evidence has in fact been lost, and perhaps I should grant Ms. Winter's motion after all."

Exactly! Talon thought. Maybe she would actually win.

"But I think there's a middle road here that addresses the defense's concerns without dismissing the entire case."

Or not.

"I am going to order," Judge Kozlowski pronounced, "that the State is prohibited from any argument, comment, cross-examination, or other mention of the time gap between the incident and Dr. Jankles's later evaluation of the defendant. With that order in place, and with the full expectation that the State will follow the orders of this Court, I am going to deny the defendant's motion to dismiss."

"So, we lost," Hunter growled at her. "Again."

"Mostly." Talon nodded. "He threw us a crumb."

Everything after that was the usual blur. The judge leaving the bench. The guards taking Hunter away. Cecilia and Riordan marching off without a word. Talon took a moment to let it all happen around her, until she was alone in the courtroom, her thoughts returning to full rationality as she accepted losing yet another well-crafted, legally supported motion. She was feeling a lot of emotions just then, but mostly, she felt tired.

The best cure for her exhaustion following the blood bath of her criminal court battle, she considered, might just be another meeting with those duplicitous civil attorneys and their offer of more money for less constant and predictable failure.

CHAPTER 26

The main Seattle office of Erickson, Larson and Sondheim was located north of downtown, in the city's trendy South Lake Union District. Most of the office buildings there were occupied by tech start-ups and tech behemoths. Apparently, the partners at EL&S wanted to be part of that shiny new community rather than the far traditional legal district surrounding the county courthouse at the far gritty south end of downtown. It suggested their litigation department didn't go to court very often. But the South Lake Union office was easy access off the Mercer Street exit from Interstate-5 and there was parking onsite, so there was that.

The longest delay of the entire trip had been the approximately 90 seconds between Talon leaving Cassandra Sondheim a voicemail about moving forward with the process and Cassandra calling her back to book the exact date and time. It seemed Talon had contacted her at the height of her interest. Then again, the same was starting to feel true for Talon.

Stepping off the elevator from the garage to the lobby, Talon admired the floor-to-vaulted-ceiling glass and steel windows that allowed natural sunlight to fill the modern and airy space. It wouldn't be a bad way to start every workday. Better than walking past the Pierce County Jail, especially if the wind was blowing the wrong way.

"Hello." Talon checked in with the receptionist in the lobby. "My name is Talon Winter. I have an appointment with Cassandra Sondheim of Er—"

"Welcome, Ms. Winter," the receptionist interrupted. "Cassandra has told me all about you. We're very excited to have you here today."

Well, that's nice, Talon supposed.

The receptionist opened a door and extracted an ID badge on a lanyard. "Here's your building pass for the day."

Talon accepted it from her and looked at it. She expected it to be generic with the word 'VISITOR' printed on it. Instead, it was personalized, with her name and the photo from her law firm website. "Uh, great. Thanks. So, should I just wait here for Ms. Sondheim or—?"

"Here she comes now," the receptionist nodded toward Cassandra approaching from the elevator banks. "Our face recognition software would have identified you when you parked your car and then sent an email to your scheduled contact person."

Talon smiled awkwardly. "Creepy."

The receptionist laughed lightly. "Nothing to worry about if you have nothing to hide."

"Is that the building motto?" Talon asked. "Or is that a line from *1984*?"

Another laugh from the receptionist but she deferred any further conversation to Cassandra who had reached the front desk.

"Talon! It's wonderful to see you again. Ready?"

Talon wasn't so sure anymore. But she said, "Sure," anyway. What was a little facial recognition software compared to twice the money and half the stress?

"Great! Come on." Cassandra grabbed the back of Talon's

elbow and turned her toward the elevators. "We don't want to keep the partners waiting."

"Oh well, no, of course not," Talon agreed, doing her best to conceal the sarcasm in her voice. She wasn't sure she'd managed it completely, but Cassandra was willing to pretend she hadn't heard it.

Erickson, Larson and Sondheim was located on floors 42, 43, and 44, Cassandra explained, with the firm's reception center on the 44th floor. "Put on your lanyard," Cassandra exhorted as the elevator came to a stop.

Talon had almost forgotten about the ID clutched in her hand. She unfurled the cord, noticed for the first time it had 'ERICKSON LARSON & SONDHEIM' woven into it, and looped it over her head, her pirated photo facing outward to double her facially recognized features as she stepped off the elevator into the lavishly decorated and dramatically lit lobby—er, 'reception center'—of her potential new employer.

There were not one, but three receptionists, all young men not more than twenty years old, with headphones over their equally stylish hair and sporting matching outfits of white dress shirts, black pants, and brightly colored ties. Two of the young men ignored Cassandra and Talon's approach, continuing on with whatever conversations they were having. The third looked up only long enough to offer Cassandra a sharp nod before returning his attention to his own call. But it wasn't as if they needed the reception boys to let them in, apparently. Cassandra led Talon to large, frosted-glass double doors and flashed her own ID badge over the reader next to them. The doors unlocked with an audible click, and Cassandra pushed one of them open. "Welcome to Erickson, Larson and Sondheim."

Not so fast, Talon thought to herself. *I still have a few questions before I join The Stepford Firm.*

"I'm sure you have a lot of questions," Cassandra seemed to read her mind, "but I really think the partners are going to agree you're just the person we're looking for."

Talon didn't get to see much of the interior of the firm because the aforementioned partners were already assembled and waiting for her in the large conference room directly across from the entrance doors. It was floor-to-ceiling glass on all four walls, with a panoramic view of Lake Union and the Seattle skyline, including the city's iconic Space Needle. Of course.

"Ms. Winter?" The man in the middle of the partners stood to greet her. He didn't bother extending a hand to shake because it never would have reached across the enormous conference table between him and his four colleagues on the one side and Talon on the other. He was late middle age, white, and a little on the heavy side. Just like everyone on the other side of the table. Once Cassandra abandoned Talon to take a seat with the rest of the firm's representatives, it made for three men and three women, all wearing conservative business suits and static smiles. "Thank you for meeting with us today. We have been looking forward to seeing you in person."

Talon frowned slightly at the awkward wording of the welcome. "Thanks. I'm glad to be here. You certainly have very nice offices."

"Do we?" the man replied, with a quick glance around. "You stop noticing after a while, I think. Nice of you to remind us. I'm Brian Larson, the managing partner. These are my colleagues representing the firm's executive, personnel, and diversity committees."

He listed off the names of the other four people Talon was faced with, but she didn't bother trying to remember them. She was more interested in hearing more details about a law firm with its own committees, especially the ones he listed. She wondered what other committees they might have. Discipline seemed likely somehow.

The rest of the meeting was short and stilted, almost awkward, like small talk at a party you didn't want to go to in the first place. They seemed to already know everything about her, maybe more than she knew herself. Her ID badge was proof they had already mined her website, but they also had statistics of how many cases she'd had over the last three years, how many trials she'd done in that same period, how many she'd won, and how many had resolved short of trial with what they termed an 'acceptably positive client-based result'. In fact, they didn't seem to have questions for her as much as they wanted her to know that they already knew what they wanted to know about her.

"Do you have any questions for us?" Larson asked, although his expression suggested he hoped she didn't.

"Yes, actually," Talon said. "Why me?"

Larson shifted in his seat and cast an uncomfortable glance at one of the women to his left. He gestured toward Cassandra. "I'm sure Ms. Sondheim has explained the reasons for our recruitment. We are seeking an experienced litigator to handle significant civil litigation in Pierce County."

"Right," Talon acknowledged. "Why me specifically? I don't even do civil. I'm a criminal defense attorney."

"You've done civil in the past," one of the other partners spoke up. She was probably a few years younger than Larson with blonde/gray hair pulled back in a pony tail. "In fact, you were with a civil firm when you handled your first criminal case, isn't that correct? A matter in the Puyallup Tribal Court, I believe."

Talon narrowed her eyes. That was an amazing, and

disconcerting, amount of detail they had on her.

"That is correct," Talon confirmed.

Before she could express her growing discomfort at their command of the details of her professional life, the same woman asked, "Are you still a member of the tribe?"

"The Puyallup Tribe?" Talon raised an eyebrow at the question. "Yeah. It's kind of a lifelong thing. They don't revoke your ancestry for not paying your annual dues or anything like that."

The woman forced a polite laugh. "Of course not. That's how it should be, of course."

"So, ahem," Larson interrupted. "Any further questions about the firm or our resources? I can assure you that you will be given the best staff and whatever resources you require. No more searching for shady so-called experts or begging clients to pay expenses."

Talon wasn't sure how to respond. Did they know all about Dr. Jankles, too, or was it just generally known that was how criminal defense attorneys operated? She doubted those lawyers in that office at that location knew very much about how real lawyers like her operated.

"I'm going to need to think about it," Talon finally said.

Larson shot a frustrated glance at Cassandra. Then almost as quickly returned an amiable expression to Talon. "Of course. It's a significant decision. But please don't take too much longer. Litigation is ongoing and deadlines are approaching. We'd really like to make you the face of our Tacoma office as soon as we possibly can."

Talon could hardly blame them for that. She was awesome.

She just needed to think it over a bit more. Maybe talk to someone about it. Not Patty; she had enough on her plate. And it needed to be someone she trusted to tell her the truth. Not just a

colleague, but a friend. And damn it, she knew who that was.
She just couldn't let Curt know it too.

CHAPTER 27

Curt was a friend, not a boyfriend. It was dinner, not a date. But it had been a while for Talon, and that near miss with Jimmy James had reminded her of that. It wasn't a date, but it wasn't completely out of the realm of remotest possibility that maybe Curt, if everything broke his way, could get lucky. But probably not.

"Thanks for grabbing dinner with me, Curt," she started the conversation after the waiter took their drink orders. It was just a beer and burger joint up the street from her office, one of several lined up next to each other that all seemed to be different versions of the same restaurant. She had to double check her texts to see which one of the three they had agreed to meet at, or she might have ended up sitting at basically the same table looking at basically the same menu, but one building over. "I have something I want to run past you."

"I'm here for you, Talon." He pointed at her with double finger guns and a wink. "Run me over with it."

That was the real risk of the evening. Running Curt over with her news and leaving him for dead in her rearview mirror. If she took the job with Erickson, Larson and Sondheim, she was pretty sure they were going to have their own investigators for whatever stupid things civil lawyers needed investigated. Bank statements or something equally boring. That meant she wouldn't be working with Curt anymore. And they both knew that would eventually mean they wouldn't see each other anymore.

"I got a job offer." Talon decided to just put it out there.

"Oh yeah?" Curt smiled for her. "Where? It's not at the public defender's office, is it? I heard they're hiring, but that's a tough way to practice. Just look at Patty. No control over who your clients are, total lack of resources. On the other hand, great benefits. And a pension. Nobody gets a pension anymore. So, it's maybe not so bad after all, I guess."

"It's not with the public defender's office," Talon answered. "It's with a private firm."

"Really? Which one?" Curt asked. "I work with a lot of the bigger defense firms in town. I can tell you the inside scoop. You know, like if you really want to work there or not. It's not Mark Hennessey's firm, is it? I hear he's a crazy boss to work for. Just totally—"

"It's not a criminal defense firm, Curt," Talon interjected.

"Oh." Curt seemed to understand what that might mean, at least at an emotional level until his brain could double check his heart's work.

"It's a civil firm," Talon continued. "A Seattle firm."

"Seattle?" Curt was never one to hide his emotions. Talon would have used the word 'crestfallen' to describe him just then. "You're moving to Seattle?"

Seattle was only 30 miles north from Tacoma, but with traffic, it could take two hours or more. It might as well have been on the other side of the state.

"No, they're opening a Tacoma office," Talon explained. "I'd be heading up the Tacoma litigation division."

"Oh, well, that's nice," Curt said. "I guess."

"Well, I mean, only if I take the job," Talon hedged. "I haven't said yes yet."

Curt ventured a hopeful grin. "I don't suppose they hire independent private investigators ever?"

Talon gave a pained smile too. "I don't suppose they probably do."

Curt forced a broader smile, but his body language betrayed his disappointment. He leaned back in his chair and nodded a few times. "Well, I mean, it makes sense. You're really good at what you do. Someone was bound to take notice one of these days. I knew you'd move on eventually. I just always figured it would be to become a judge or something."

Talon burst out laughing. "A judge? Me? Um, no. No, thank you."

"I think you'd be a great judge," Curt defended.

Talon shook her head. "I don't know about that."

"You care about what's right," Curt said.

"I care about winning," Talon corrected him. "That's part of why I'm tempted to take this new job. I'm sick of always banging my head against the wall and having nothing to show for it."

"Nothing might be okay. You'd normally have blood running down your face to show for that," Curt suggested.

"That's exactly what it feels like some days," Talon said. "It doesn't matter how hard I work, or how crooked the cops are, or how strong the law is on my side, I still lose. Not because of me, but because of my clients, and what they did. Justice is supposed to be blind, but that lady with the sword is peeking out from under the blindfold when it's a criminal case, even the serious ones. Especially the serious ones. Just once I'd like to win because I'm right."

"That all makes sense," Curt voiced his support. Of course. "This way, you can use your talents and abilities to help other people. Rich people. And corporations. Rich corporations. Rich people and rich corporations. But they're always the good guys, right?"

Talon couldn't help but smile. "I see what you're doing, Mr. Fairchild."

Curt played innocent, turning up his palms. "I'm not doing anything, Ms. Winter. Just sharing what little knowledge I have of that branch of the legal profession."

"Uh huh," Talon crossed her arms. "I'm sure your motives are pure."

"Completely selfless," Curt assured.

The waiter returned with their drinks then. Curt got whatever the latest featured local microbrew was. Talon got a glass of red wine. It would pair well with the medium-rare cheeseburger she knew she was going to order when the waiter returned.

"So, what firm is it?" Curt asked. "I might know something about them. Probably not, but maybe."

"Erickson, Larson and Sondheim," Talon answered. "To be honest, I'd never heard of them until I was approached by their recruiter a few weeks ago."

"Erickson, Larson and Sondheim?" Curt repeated. "Yeah, I think I've heard of them. They're handling some big case down here."

"They are?" Talon leaned forward. "That's probably the case they want to hire me for. The old partner dude today said something about upcoming deadlines."

"Yeah, it's kind of a big deal, I think," Curt pursed his lips and glanced at the ceiling as he tried to recall the details. "The Commencement Bay Yacht Club is getting sued to get the land back.

There's a lot of really rich and really powerful Tacomans who have boats moored at the Commencement Bay Yacht Club."

"Wait, back up." Talon raised a hand at him. "Did you say they're getting sued to get the land back? Get the land back to who? Who's suing them to get the land back?"

Curt's eyes widened in realization, even as Talon already knew the answer. "The Tribe," he confirmed. "The Puyallup Tribe is suing to get back a small portion of their ancestral lands."

Talon shoved back in her seat as she pushed the bile back down her throat. "And they want my Puyallup Indian face to be the face of their firm."

CHAPTER 28

Talon considered every possible way to tell Cassandra Sondheim and the rest of Erickson, Larson and Motherfuckers to go fuck themselves. Everything from a single-worded text of 'No' to Cassandra followed by ghosting, to storming their Seattle offices ready to kick ass and take names. She'd give their facial recognition software a reason to remember her face over and above its Native ancestry.

Then there was everything in between, from a formal email detailing her personal and professional displeasure with their scheme, to meeting with Cassandra and just telling her the truth and expressing her disappointment at almost being used like that.

In the end, she opted for what made the most sense for her right there and right then. She didn't do anything. The longer they thought she and her beautiful Native American face might actually front the effort to deprive her own tribe of their own land, the less time they would have to fill the position when they finally realized she wasn't coming on board, and the closer those deadlines would be when that other lawyer, whoever they might be, finally took over the litigation mid-battle.

Besides, Talon had real work to do. Hunter's trial was just

over a week away. There was a lot to do. Cassandra Sondheim and her law firm had been a distraction. Without that distraction, she could focus her attention fully on Hunter's case and bring to bear the full force of her talents, skills, abilities, industriousness, and insatiable desire to win, all for the lofty and noble goal of tricking a jury into walking a heartless double murderer out the door.

A lot of the final trial prep was putting pieces of paper together. Witness lists and exhibit lists. Photographs and witness statements. Police reports and autopsy reports and expert reports. All of them copied and printed and filed into binders, to be available at Talon's fingertips in case she suddenly needed any of them during the course of the trial. Lawyers dealt with paper. But trial lawyers also dealt with people. So, the other part of trial prep was one last round with the other principal players in the trial.

First stop, the Pierce County Prosecutor's Office.

"Hello," Talon greeted the latest receptionist in the prosecutor's office lobby. "I'm here to speak with Mr. Riordan."

The receptionist smiled a tight smile. "Do you have an appointment?"

"I do actually," Talon reported. She wasn't going to just show up and expect to speak to the chief of the entire criminal division without an appointment. Not again. "My name is Talon Winter. It's regarding the Burgess case."

If the receptionist knew the case by name, she didn't show it. Instead, she looked to her monitor and clicked her mouse a few times. "Yes. I see it here. But unfortunately, Mr. Riordan is unavailable. Something came up. That happens a lot, actually. I'm sure you understand."

Talon did not understand, but she wasn't surprised either.

"Is Ms. Thompson available?" she asked.

"Cecilia Thompson, Brenda Thompson, or Tiffani

Thompson?"

That was a lot of Thompsons. "Cecilia."

"Let me check." The receptionist clicked her mouse a few more times. "You're in luck. Looks like she just got back from court. Let me send her an instant message."

Talon supposed that probably sounded cutting edge a decade or so ago, but she appreciated the effort.

A moment later, the receptionist's computer beeped, and she announced, "Ms. Thompson will be right out."

'Right out' meant more like five full minutes, but eventually Cecilia emerged into the lobby.

"Talon." She put a hand on her hip. "What are you doing here?"

"Trial's next week," Talon explained. "I thought we should talk one more time and see if there isn't a way to resolve it."

Cecilia waited a moment, then frowned. "Is he gonna plead guilty to two counts of murder in the first degree?"

"Um. No," Talon answered.

"Okay, great talk, Talon." Cecilia started to turn around. "See you next week."

"Really? That's it?"

Cecilia turned around. "I mean, yeah. He killed his grandparents, right? And like, really, really brutally. What do you expect? A dismissal and an apology letter? Sorry, Talon, if you want a dismissal, you'll have to get that from the judge. Oh, wait. You already did that. How did that go for you again?"

Okay, Talon thought, *I tried. Did my due diligence. Time to go.*

"You're right. The judge didn't throw the case out," Talon answered. "Guess I'll just have to get the jury to do it."

CHAPTER 29

Brave talk. Talon was good at that. But there was one problem: her client was guilty as sin.

The final bit of trial prep was always one last meeting with the client. It was important to explain procedures and manage expectations. Mostly so she didn't have a client constantly grabbing her arm and whispering in her ear as she tried to pay attention to the proceedings and find that one path through the eye of the needle to a 'not guilty' verdict. Not only was it annoying, but that sort of nervous behavior was sketchy as hell and the jury would definitely notice.

Trial was scheduled to start first thing Monday morning. So, Sunday afternoon, Talon made her way to the jail and passed through the security systems until she found herself one last time sitting in a jail conference room with Hunter Burgess. After this, all of their conversations would take place in the courtroom. At least until after the trial, when she came to visit him before his sentencing hearing.

"Ms. Winter," Hunter greeted her as the guard pushed him inside. A little rougher than last time. Talon wondered whether Hunter had started acting up or if his personality was just finally getting to even the most calloused guards. "Are we ready for tomorrow?"

"I am," Talon answered. She was already seated at the small plastic table. She had her back to the wall and didn't stand up when Hunter came in. He took the seat opposite her. "How are you feeling?"

"I feel quite well, actually," Hunter answered, "considering the circumstances. I always knew it would come to this. Now comes the last act of the drama."

That was one way to think of it, Talon supposed.

"I don't know how much court television you've watched," Talon said, "but it's a lot more boring than what they show on T.V. There's a lot of downtime, and things take forever, and we spend a lot of time arguing about the rules instead of what actually happened."

"But we will talk about what actually happened, correct?" Hunter asked. "It's been so long. I've started to forget, if you can believe that. Not all of it, of course, but some of the details. I want to remember all of the details."

"Oh yeah, we'll be talking about what happened," Talon assured him. "At least the prosecutors will. That's kind of their main job. Mine is to talk about anything but that."

Hunter leaned back and folded his hands in his lap. "That's fine."

Glad you approve, Talon thought to herself.

"One thing you need to understand," she continued, "is that the jury is going to be watching you constantly. Not all of them all of the time, but at least one of them at any given moment. They are going to decide whether they believe you could have done this."

"Oh, I did it," Hunter interjected.

"Yeah, I know," Talon answered. "Not the point. They don't

know if you did it, and ultimately that's the question they have to decide, so they are going to look around for any information they can find to help them make that decision. Humans gather a lot of information about each other from nonverbal cues, probably more than we do from what people actually say. When someone tells us something, we look at their facial expressions, posture, body language, eye contact, all of that to decide whether to believe them and to gauge what the other person's emotions are, to whatever extent that may be relevant. They aren't going to get to observe you talking, so they're going to watch every move you make while you're sitting in the courtroom."

Hunter frowned. "What do you mean they won't get to observe me talking? What about when I testify?"

Talon couldn't help but laugh at that. "Oh, you're not testifying. There is no way I can put you on the stand."

"Why not?" Hunter whined. "It's my decision."

"And it's your ass that will go to prison for the rest of your life if you take the stand," Talon explained. "If you testify, they will absolutely know you did it, and everything else I'm going to do will be a complete waste of my time and effort."

"But I want to talk to the jurors," Hunter protested. "The only people I've been able to talk to about the case are you and that weird doctor."

"Larry, yeah," Talon acknowledged. "Well, there are reasons for that."

"What reasons?"

"Well, number one," Talon counted off her fingers, "you're guilty. Number two, when you talk about it, it's obvious you're guilty. And number three, it's my job to get the jury to say, 'not guilty,' despite numbers one and two."

"I'll just tell them I didn't do it," Hunter said. "I can be very convincing."

"No, you can't," Talon told him. "Trust me. I've been doing this a while now. I know convincing. You're not it. And I can tell that in a private conversation like this. Put you on display on the witness stand getting cross-examined by a prosecutor who's been convicting murderers since before you were born, and you'll be drawing a diagram for the jury about exactly how you delivered each blow."

Hunter didn't say anything, but his mouth curled into a smile at the edges.

"See?" Talon pointed at him. "That. That is why you're not testifying. Not only are they going to hate you—which is enough for them to convict you—but they're going to be scared of you. And if they're scared of you, they will absolutely, positively, one-hundred-percent-guaranteed send you to prison for the rest of your life."

Hunter nodded at that and let his smile take over his lips fully. "Are *you* afraid of me?"

"Nah." Talon laughed darkly and waved off the suggestion. "I'm not your grandparents."

CHAPTER 30

The night before trial was its own thing, and it was always the same thing. There wasn't anything left to do, but it wasn't possible to relax either. Talon wasn't worried, but she was anxious. Anxious to get started, anxious to execute, anxious to win. A double murder trial was a big deal. If she wasn't anxious, she wasn't paying attention.

She didn't mind sitting in her condo, sipping a single glass of wine and letting her brain wander over the details of her trial strategy. There were worse ways to spend an evening. But she also knew she needed to get some rest and would soon need a distraction to break through the mental stress loop, lest that loop start spiraling and leave her unable to get the sleep she would need to perform her best the next day.

But not just any distraction.

Her phone buzzed and she looked at the caller ID. It was Patty. 8:15 on a Sunday night. But Talon just couldn't. She needed to stay focused on her case, and Patty had just been too much drama lately. Talon could call her back after she got the first day of trial under her belt. Whatever it was, Talon was sure it could wait. She watched the screen until the call went to voicemail, then she leaned back and closed her eyes again, trying to relax.

It didn't work. Patty's call reminded her of the last time Patty interrupted her plans. All for the good, as it turned out. But part of those plans would have been fun regardless of the ultimate outcome of her flirtation with Erickson, Larson and Sondheim. Or maybe because of that outcome. James was never going to be her boss after all, so he could have at least been a one-time conquest.

Thoughts of that missed opportunity weren't helping her relax. If anything, they were having the opposite effect. She knew she needed to get some rest, and the call from Patty had reminded her of at least one way to break through and be able to relax. It wouldn't be the first time it had worked the night before trial. And despite the complications it would undoubtedly bring later, she was dedicated enough to her job to be willing to try it again.

She picked up her phone and texted Curt.

Booty call?

It was probably too direct, but it was getting late. And she'd finished that glass of wine already.

She watched her phone for a reply. It took longer than it should have but eventually she could see that Curt was typing.

Then it went away.

Then he was typing again.

Then it went away again.

Then more typing and finally a response.

Go to bed, Talon.

Talon frowned. He wasn't supposed to turn her down.

Then he added a few more texts:

By yourself, I mean.

Not with me.

Obviously.

A pause, then, *Good luck tomorrow.*

Another pause, then more typing, but it went away again, and then no more messages.

Talon stared at the phone for another minute or two to see if he might change his mind. He didn't.

So, she followed his advice. Nothing like a little humiliation to make you want to pull the covers over your head. It was probably just as well. She had a big day tomorrow.

CHAPTER 31

Much like the night before the first day of trial, the first day
of trial itself was its own thing. It was the first crack in the egg. Not
all that much actually happened; there were too many procedural
and housekeeping details to take care of first to get anywhere near
the merits of the case. But the trial of a thousand steps had to start
with a single call to order by the bailiff.

"All rise! The Pierce County Superior Court is now in
session, The Honorable Jerry Kozlowski presiding."

Talon shook her head slightly at the 'Jerry'. Maybe she
should let Jankles call himself 'Larry' after all. Big trial, with Tally
against Ronny and Ceely, to see if Hunty murdered Granny and
Grampy.

Just kidding, of course. He definitely did.

"Are the parties ready for trial in the matter of *The State of
Washington versus Hunter Burgess*?"

"The State is ready, Your Honor," Riordan stood to answer.

Talon stood as well and surveyed the courtroom. Hunter
was seated next to her, dressed in a suit, so the jury wouldn't know
he was being held in jail pending the outcome of the trial. Nothing
cast doubt on that whole 'presumed innocent' thing like a judge

putting someone in jail before the trial. The jurors might figure it out anyway, though, based on the presence of the uniformed guards at every exit especially given the nature of the charges.

Riordan was still standing at the table next to hers. Cecilia was seated and facing forward as if consciously trying not to look at Talon.

In the gallery behind them sat Chad Burgess, but only him. Not Karen. The prosecution and Talon had both endorsed Karen as a witness, and witnesses weren't allowed to listen to the testimony of other witnesses. The danger was that they would adjust their testimony, either intentionally or unconsciously. Talon had expected Karen to protest when she explained it to her, but she had seemed relieved. Chad would be happy to watch for both of them, he'd said. And Karen was happy to let him, although she left it unspoken.

Talon turned back to look up at the judge. "The defense is ready, Your Honor," she confirmed.

And they were off.

The first matter was scheduling. Days and hours in session, schedule conflicts, lunch for the jurors and the defendant (back at the jail). The next matter was motions *in limine*, the simple evidentiary rulings the judge needed to lay down before they got started in earnest. Judge Kozlowski reminded the State that they couldn't attack the gap in time between the murders and Dr. Jankles's evaluation, although they were welcome to attack any other aspect of it, which they undoubtedly would. No hearsay, obviously. No witnesses giving opinions about the truthfulness of other witnesses. The rules that applied to every case, but needed to be confirmed beforehand anyway, just to be sure everyone understood how to play fair. But even those simple preliminary matters took the better part of a full day. Lawyers talked. A lot.

Four lawyers, counting the judge, talked all day.

The next matter to address was selecting the jury. That took a lot longer than scheduling, although there was an aspect of scheduling to that too. They only needed twelve jurors, but to get to that number, they brought in a panel of 100 potential jurors. A murder case was a lengthy time commitment. Everyone on that panel had committed to two weeks of jury duty, as stated in the jury summons they received. Not all of them could stay on a jury for the two months or more a murder trial could take. Those jurors who couldn't were excused right at the beginning, and the panel went from a fairly representative cross section of the community to a group dominated by teachers who would keep their jobs no matter how long they were gone from them and retirees who didn't have jobs they needed to get back to. Talon could live with the teachers, but she was pretty sure the retirees were going to sympathize more with grandma and grandpa than they would with little Hunter.

The attorneys had the opportunity to ask questions of the jurors, but they were strictly prohibited from sharing any facts from the case or asking what types of evidence they would need to convict or acquit. So, basically the questioning was worthless. Instead, it focused on whether they would follow the law (of course they would) and insipid questions about favorite books and last movie seen in order to glean some sort of feeling as to what type of person any particular potential juror might be.

In the end, Talon struck six people she didn't like from the panel, and the prosecutors did the same, and the next twelve in line became the jury. Talon didn't love them, but she didn't hate them, and she supposed that was all she could ask for really.

Once the jurors were selected, Judge Kozlowski had them stand and raise their right hands so he could administer their oath. Would they 'well and truly try the case with an earnest desire to reach a proper verdict?' Of course, they would. Too bad for Talon.

It was late in the afternoon by the time the jurors were sworn in and there was a strong disfavor of allowing only one side to give their opening statement then adjourning for the night. The jurors might mull on the accusations of the State without having yet heard the counter argument from the defense. So, Judge Kozlowski sent the jurors home a little early, confirmed there was nothing else to be addressed before opening statements the next morning, then adjourned the case for the day.

Hunter was taken back to the jail. Chad left the courtroom. Riordan and Cecilia went back to their offices. And Talon went home to eat dinner, maybe drink a small glass of wine, not text Curt, and get a good night's sleep.

Too bad that didn't happen.

CHAPTER 32

Talon stepped inside her condo, flipped the light on, locked the door behind her, and tossed the keys on her dining table. It had been a long day, a long few days actually. She was glad for the extra hours Kozlowski had given them with the early adjournment. She was going to pour an early drink and put her feet up while she went over her planned opening statement one more time. Well, probably more than one time. It didn't have to be perfect, but it was going to be. That's why she was the best, or so they said.

That reminded Talon. She poured that drink and made her way to the sofa, kicking her shoes off on the way. She plopped down and pulled out her phone. Time to check her voicemails. It had turned into a nightly routine, one that brought a smile to her face.

'Hi, Talon. It's Cassandra again. Cassandra Sondheim. Please give me a call when you get the chance. Thanks.'

Talon took a sip from her glass and pressed 'DELETE' on her phone, causing the next voicemail to play.

'Talon. It's Cassandra Sondheim. Please call me.'

DELETE

'Hey, Talon. It's Cassandra. How are you doing? Hey, look, I

happen to them. And we're the only ones who can help them. But half the time, they don't even appreciate it. No one does. No one appreciates what we do. Everyone hates us. Do you see how people look at you when you tell them what you do for a living? Nobody ever asks Jeff how he can do what he does, but every person I tell I'm a defense attorney always asks, 'Oh my God, how can you do that?' like I'm murdering kittens or something. Usually, I just smile and say something about everyone deserving a defense, but sometimes I just want to scream at them. Do you know why cops can't just bust into your house and search for those drugs we both know you keep in your underwear drawer? Because they did that to some poor kid who lived in the wrong neighborhood and someone like me fought it and took it all the way to the fucking Supreme Court and they said you can't do that. Do you know why they can't ask you questions without telling you that you have the right to a lawyer first? Do you know why they can't just pull your car over and search it for fun? Why you can do and say and think what you want without fear the government will take your life and just rip it apart? Because of someone like me. Someone you look down on and pity and hate who did their job anyway and you don't even know. But it's not just that, it's everything. There's just so. Much. Pressure. All the time. And I'm not even talking about the clients or the judges or even the prosecutor. I'm talking about the rest of the fucking criminal defense bar. Not you, maybe, Talon, but everyone else, it seems like. This job is so hard and so thankless, it's like we have to keep cheering each other on. Rah, rah. Doing God's work or whatever. But it never ends. You have to be a true believer and you have to do it twenty-four/seven, seven days a week, fifty-two weeks a year. It's like if you're not constantly on and working for your clients, you're letting The Man win. But damn it, Talon, sometimes I just want to take my son to the park. God knows Jeff won't do it after a long week of doing nothing important. But if I go to the park with Jack for an hour, then that's an hour I wasn't fighting The System, an hour I wasn't giving my very soul to every fucking client in the jail, an hour that if I'd spent it on work I might have finally seen the one tiny little weakness in the State's case that would let me get my client an acquittal. But I didn't see it. And now he's going to be convicted. All because I took time for myself. Because there's never time for yourself. And it's never enough anyway. Because they're all guilty anyway. And that's why everyone hates us. And that's why I really wanted to talk to you tonight, Talon, because I just don't think I can do this anymore.

'I know I can't do this anymore.

'I'm not going to this anymore.

'Goodbye, Talon.'

"Oh fuck." Talon didn't delete the message. She tapped on Patty's name to pull up her contact info and pressed 'CALL' as soon as it came up.

"Come on, Patty. Answer."

One ring.

Two rings.

Three rings.

Four rings.

Voicemail.

"Fuck!" Talon ended the call and tried again.

Ring. Ring. Ring. Ring. Voicemail.

"Fuck, fuck, fuck."

She jumped off the sofa and started pulling up Patty's text with her address even as she chased down her shoes, grabbed her keys off the table, and rushed out into the darkening evening.

CHAPTER 33

Talon drove as fast as she could while also looking at the map on her phone and being sure not to run any stop signs or red lights. Running a red could cause an accident, and she didn't want to run off the road while looking at her phone, but the worst speeding would do is get a cop to light her up. And if that happened, good. They could follow her to Patty's house.

Except, Talon saw, as she approached the address, they were already there.

"Oh, no."

The sun had almost fully set by then, and Patty's home was lit up by the red and blue strobe of the three police cars parked in front of it. Talon slammed on her brakes and came to a skidding halt behind the last of them. She jumped out, the car still lurching forward, and sprinted over the grass as best she could in her work heels. When she reached the front door, one of the cops finally noticed her and reached out before she could push past him through the front door.

"Whoa!" the burly man called out as he grabbed her. "Hold on! This is a police scene. You can't go inside without authorization. Who are you?"

"I'm a friend," Talon panted. "A friend of Patty's."

The officer's response of, "Oh," confirmed Talon's worst fear.

"You have to let me in," Talon pleaded. "I'm her friend. I'm an attorney. She called me. She called me and left a voicemail. I'm a criminal defense attorney, and I'm her friend, and you have to let me inside."

The officer's grip softened a bit, but he didn't let go of her completely. "I'm sorry, ma'am."

"Sorry for what?" Talon demanded. "Sorry for not letting me in or for—?" She didn't finish her thought. But she didn't have to.

"Did you say you were an attorney?" the cop asked.

"Yes," Talon confirmed. "I do criminal. Murders. I've seen everything. Let me inside."

"Are you the family's lawyer?" the cop almost suggested.

"Sure," Talon took the suggestion. "I'm the family's lawyer. They called me. I'm here. Let me inside."

"Hold on a second," the cop said. He let go of her, in part because he trusted her not to just run inside, but mostly so he could turn away while he called over his shoulder-mounted radio. "I've got an attorney out here. What's your name again, ma'am?"

"Talon Winter," she answered even as she craned her neck to see inside. But there was nothing in view from the front porch.

"Right," the cop said. Then again into his radio, "Can you confirm with the husband that attorney Talon Winter can come inside? Over."

A few moments later, another voice came over the porch cop's radio. "Affirmative. She can enter. Tell her to go straight to the kitchen. Stay out of the bedroom."

The cop turned to relay the instruction to Talon, but there was no need.

"I heard." And she rushed inside.

The kitchen was straight through the living room, another uniformed officer already waving her to come directly over. She wouldn't have been able to go to the bedroom anyway. The hallway to the bedrooms was blocked by a throng of cops and forensic officers. She knew what that meant. She knew as soon as Patty's voicemail ended.

Jeff was in the kitchen. Distraught wasn't a strong enough word. Destroyed was more like it.

He looked up at her, recognizing her as Patty's friend only because she clearly wasn't one of the cops who'd responded when he'd called 911 after coming home to find Patty's body and the suicide note on the nightstand.

She'd died alone.

"Why?" he asked her. "Why did she do it? I don't understand. I don't know why. Do you know why?"

Talon knew why. But she also didn't know. It didn't make sense, except it also did. Nothing really mattered. But this did. To Jeff. To Jack. But not to Patty. Not enough. It was everything she'd said in her voicemail, and more, and none of that. It was senseless and only logical. And Talon could only think it had been avoidable, if only she'd answered her phone.

CHAPTER 34

It was a long, terrible, powerless night. Talon didn't stay long to comfort Jeff; she barely knew him. And she had nothing of value to offer the cops. She just drove home again. Alone. In the dark. And sat in the living room of her condo. Alone in the dark.

At some point she must have moved to the bedroom because she woke up in her bed, the alarm on her phone showing no regard for the life lost the previous evening.

And her phone wouldn't be the only one. Judge Kozlowski had a jury ready to hear opening statements. He wasn't likely to delay the proceedings because some lawyer not directly involved in the trial had happened to kill herself the night before. And Riordan would be an even bigger jerk about it. Talon knew if she asked, she'd get a day. One day. But what would that one day give her? Nothing. Just another night wondering what might have happened if she didn't always keep her phone on silent and never checked her voicemails until the end of the day. What might have happened if having five voicemails was an alert that something was wrong, rather than a joke at Cassandra Sondheim's expense. And, ultimately, at Patty Rodgers's expense as well.

No. She would put on her big lawyer panties and march into

that courtroom like she owned the damn place, just like she did every other day. No one would know how or even whether the events of the previous evening had affected her. She was Talon Winter, damn it. She was the best.

So, the next morning, everyone assembled again in Judge Kozlowski's courtroom. Talon didn't greet anyone, and no one tried to greet her. The bailiff called the courtroom to order, and the judge took the bench. The jurors filed out of the jury room and took their seats in the jury box. Judge Kozlowski welcomed them, and began the trial in earnest.

"Ladies and gentlemen of the jury," he instructed them, "please give your attention to Mr. Riordan who will now deliver the opening statement on behalf of the State of Washington."

Chief Criminal Prosecutor Ronald Riordan stood up from his seat behind the prosecution table. He had taken the seat closer to the jury, of course. He buttoned his suit coat, then stepped out into the well of the courtroom, the empty space between the jury and the judge, the witness box and the counsel table. It was the stage for the attorneys, and Riordan loved the spotlight.

"Thank you, Your Honor," he said over his shoulder toward the judge. His eyes were fixed on the jurors in front of him. He took a position directly in front of the middle of the box, not too close and not too far away. He didn't need to play games to get their attention; he had it. His would be the first words of the actual battle. Everyone was hanging on those words. Even Talon. Especially Talon. She was the only one who had to respond to them.

Talon wondered how he would start.

"A baseball bat," Riordan declared into the silence. "The defendant murdered his grandparents with a baseball bat."

Strong start, Talon had to admit.

"He beat his grandfather to death with a baseball bat,"

Riordan continued, "and he beat his grandmother to death with a baseball bat. And when the police arrived, they found the defendant, standing in the front entryway of his grandparents' home, holding that baseball bat, and covered in his grandparents' blood."

That did sound bad, Talon had to admit.

Riordan probably could have stopped at that point. That really was the entire case. They would call witnesses, of course. They had to. That whole burden of proof beyond a reasonable doubt thing. But they would all just be lending support around the edges to the basic facts of the case as Riordan had just stated them. But of course, Riordan wasn't going to stop talking. For one thing, the jury would think that was a strangely short opening statement. For another, he was a lawyer.

"Now, ladies and gentlemen, this case is both easy and difficult. It's easy because there really is no doubt about what happened that night. The defendant bludgeoned his own elderly grandparents to death for no apparent reason other than the sick joy it gave him. But it will be difficult too. Because in order to hold the defendant responsible for what he did, we have to prove to you that he did it. And in order to do that, we have to talk about what he did, and we have to show you what he did. We have to talk about it in disturbing detail, and we have to show you photographs of the aftermath. It's not enough for me to just stand here and assert the defendant murdered his grandparents with a baseball bat—"

Talon wondered how many times he was going to say that.

"—we have to call witnesses, like the medical examiner who will tell you exactly what blunt force trauma means, where he found evidence of it on the victims' bodies, and specifically, very specifically, how those injuries resulted in each victim dying."

Riordan nodded in sympathy with the jurors he imagined he

was scaring. "There will be photographs from the autopsies to help explain how an object striking the outside of a human body can cause damage to the deepest interior of the body. But those won't be the most disturbing photographs. The most disturbing photographs will be from the crime scene itself. You will see exactly how it looked to the first officers who arrived on scene, the first officers who walked into that bedroom and saw the absolute carnage the defendant caused. You'll see how hard it was to even locate the victims at first because the room was so covered in blood and—and I hate to be indelicate, but this is a murder trial, and we are required to deal with the truth here—covered in blood and brain matter and cast-off hair and teeth and even fragments of bone.

"Ladies and gentlemen, it was horrific, and I would apologize for having to show it to you, but it's necessary. It's necessary because in order to hold the defendant responsible for what he did, you have to know what he did, and you have to know why those officers were heroes for getting there so fast they caught the defendant before he could escape. Because if he had gotten away, whoever would have believed a grandson could do that to his own grandparents? But when you see the photographs of how bloody that room was, you'll understand how important the photographs of the defendant taken that night are. You'll see him covered in blood, his grandparents' blood. And you'll know it was because he was the one who splattered that blood all over his grandparents' room and himself."

Riordan took a breath, as if even he was having trouble with the weighty responsibility they all shared to hold a murderer accountable for his heinous deeds. It was also a signal that he was about to wrap up. There were only so many times you could say 'he beat his grandparents to death with a baseball bat' and Riordan had pretty much reached the limit.

"So, ladies and gentlemen, by the time we have reached the end of this trial, you will have made it through the difficult part of the trial: having to see and hear about a horrific, unforgiveable crime. But then you will be ready to do the easy part. Hold the criminal responsible. At the end of this trial, we will stand up before you again and ask you to return the only verdict that will be supported by the facts and the law. We will ask you to find the defendant guilty of two counts of murder in the first degree. Thank you."

Riordan turned, a bit dramatically Talon thought, and strode purposefully back to his seat at the prosecution table where Cecilia dutifully congratulated him on a predictably excellent opening statement.

Then it was Talon's turn.

"Ladies and gentlemen of the jury," Judge Kozlowski announced, "please give your attention now to Ms. Winter, who will deliver the opening statement on behalf of the defendant."

CHAPTER 35

Talon stood up and made her way around the counsel table to position herself in front of the jury. She didn't walk slowly exactly, but she didn't hurry either. She'd prepared her opening long ago. She had started thinking about it before she'd even finished the first consultation with the Burgesses. Each conversation with Hunter, each exchange with Cecilia and Riordan, each motion hearing and argument and late night spent reviewing the police reports yet again—each of those refined the presentation until finally, after the trial began and the jury was picked and she was confident she knew everything she could possibly know about the case, it coalesced into the perfect opening statement, informed by expertise and fueled by her never-ending desire to win.

She didn't give that opening statement.

Instead, she just talked to them. Like they were human beings with all of the same desires and insecurities as everyone else, including, she knew, herself. A human being who had been born alone, and who would die alone. Just like everyone else.

It might not be what she planned to say from the beginning, but it was what she wanted to say right then.

"A man goes for a walk," she began. She kept herself rooted before the jurors. She wasn't much of a pacer anymore—all new attorneys paced when they spoke to the jury, without even realizing it in most cases—but to whatever extent she might have tried to weave into her narrative a short stroll to one side or a step toward the jury box, she wasn't interested in those games. Not right then. Her words would carry her.

"It's a nice day," she continued to the puzzled expressions of the jurors. "Sunny, but not too hot. There's a light breeze and the trees overhead provide plenty of shade. There's the sound of birds in the distance and the rustling of leaves, but nothing too loud and it's not distracting. The man is able to lose himself in the walk because it's comfortable and pleasant, and he trusts the path he's on. He's never walked that path before, but he's heard of it from others, and everyone agrees it's a very nice path."

Talon was half-expecting an objection from Riordan, if only because he certainly had no idea what she was talking about. No one did. But that was okay. The jurors were curious where she was going with it, which meant they were paying attention.

"Eventually the trees give way, and he enters a meadow," Talon continued. "The meadow is nice, too, but not quite as nice as the forest. There are wildflowers, but the sun is hotter, and there's no shade, and there's an unpleasant sound in the distance, like a freeway. Something that breaks the spell a little bit. But the man walks on.

"There's not a path anymore either," she explained, "so the man's steps are a bit harder as he pushes through the tall grass. Soon, the wildflowers give way to just grass, and then the grass gives way to dirt, and the man finds himself on the other side of the meadow, standing before a large ravine, a chasm even. It's too steep and too deep to climb down, and it stretches out to either side for as far as the eye can see."

Talon took a moment then. Not so much a dramatic pause, but because she wanted to make sure she explained the next part correctly.

"The only way across would be a bridge. In fact, it looks like someone was planning to build a bridge. There's a pair of wooden posts, about waist high, on his side of the chasm, and another set directly across on the other side of the chasm. But there's no bridge yet.

"The man peers across the chasm and sees a beautiful, pristine lake, with water running down from the mountains and the sunlight glimmering off its surface. The man realizes he is very thirsty, and he would really like to drink some water from the lake. But he can't get across.

"Then another man walks out of the woods behind him and approaches the chasm. 'See that lake over there? You should go there.'

"'I want to,' says the first man, 'except there's no bridge.'"

'You see the water, don't you?' asks the second man. 'It's right there. That's where you should go.'

"'Yes, I see it,' the first man says, 'and I want to go there. However, I can't get there from here.'

"'Go anyway,' says the second man."

Talon paused again. That was the end of her story.

She opened her hands to the jury. "That's all of us. Every day. We're that first man, minding our own business, trying to enjoy life, and trying to adjust to the changes life gives us. Sometimes, a lot of times, we see the things we want, but we can't quite get there. We know we need bridges but sometimes the bridges just aren't there. Chasms open up between us and our goals, our friends, our families, even ourselves. The desire for a bridge still isn't a bridge, no matter how strong that desire is."

Talon took a moment to look at the two counsel tables. Hunter was staring at her like she was as crazy as he was. Cecilia looked embarrassed for her. And Riordan couldn't suppress his shit-eating grin. *Well, open up, Ronny, here comes another bite.*

Talon turned back to the jurors. "That's also the prosecution's case. They can't get there from here. They know it. But they want you to ignore that there's no bridge and walk out into the chasm."

Talon could almost hear Riordan's smile fall off his face.

"Mr. Riordan just gave you a vivid and visceral description of the forest and the meadow, and he told you he'd meet you at the waterfall, but he skipped over the fact that there's no bridge from here to there.

"Yes, Arnold and Florence Grovequist were murdered brutally, savagely, in their own bed. Yes, their grandson, Hunter Burgess, was found shortly thereafter inside their home—a home where he, too, had a bedroom. But those two things don't build the bridge to the guilty verdict Mr. Riordan is hoping you'll give him.

"There are no witnesses to what actually happened that night," Talon continued. "And there are no witnesses who can or will say Hunter was responsible for what happened to his grandparents. There is no bridge between Hunter on this side of the chasm and a verdict of guilty on the other side. No matter how badly Mr. Riordan wants there to be. And no matter how badly you might want there to be."

If any of the jurors had stopped listening to her, that accusation of bias got their attention again. But Talon wasn't about to sit down without attacking the unspoken prejudices all jurors held against criminal defendants. Otherwise, they'd be only too happy to step into the chasm for Mr. Riordan.

"From the time each of you first walked into this courtroom as a potential juror until the time you've heard all of the evidence and arguments and completed your jury service, the judge is going to tell you literally dozens of times that a criminal defendant is presumed innocent, that the State has the burden of proving the defendant is guilty, and that they have to prove it beyond any and all reasonable doubt. The judge will tell you again and again that a defendant has no burden to put forward any evidence, that he doesn't have to testify, and that if he doesn't testify you absolutely may not use his silence against him."

Those admonitions were littered throughout the form jury instructions every judge read to the juries in every criminal case.

"And do you know why the judge is going to tell you all those things so many times?" Talon asked. "Because none of you believe it. And you still won't believe it, even after the judge tells you. So, he keeps telling you, over and over again, in the hopes that you might actually let go of what you really think of criminals and actually give a defendant the fair trial he's supposed to get under the Constitution."

To a person, the jurors looked shocked to be called out like that. But for a few of them, the expression of shock seemed to melt into one of begrudging acceptance.

"None of you want to live in a country where innocent people are prosecuted for crimes they didn't commit," Talon told them. "That means you want to believe Hunter did it."

"All of you think if you were innocent, you would proclaim your innocence from the rooftops," Talon said. "That means you'll think Hunter is guilty if he doesn't testify."

"And all of you want to do your civic duty as jurors and think the other public servants in this case are the heroic prosecutors," Talon continued. "That means you want to give them a conviction before you've even heard the evidence."

"But finally, you all want to make the right decision," Talon offered. "That's what you want the most. That's why you're trying to sneak in your beliefs before you came here. Most defendants are guilty. Most innocent people say they didn't do it. Most prosecutors are heroes and most defense attorneys—well, how can they even do that job?"

She shook her head at Patty's too-true words.

"You are going to use those prejudices to help you make what you hope is the right decision," Talon told them. "That's why the judge keeps telling you not to. And that's why each and every one of you breathed a sigh of relief when Mr. Riordan told you it was an easy case. You really want to do the right thing, and you really, really want it to be easy to know what the right thing is.

"But that's not how life works.

"Life isn't easy. It isn't simple. And a criminal trial with two counts of murder in the first degree is as far from easy as you're going to get. This case will not be easy for you. Not if you do your jobs. Not if you keep your oaths. Because at the end of the trial, Mr. Riordan is going to walk out of the woods and tell you to just cross the chasm to a guilty verdict, but he won't have built you the bridge you need to get there. It won't be easy to do the right thing, because you think defendants are guilty and prosecutors are heroes. But at the end of the trial, I will stand before you again. I will point out that the prosecution has completely failed to build the bridge between the evidence they have and the verdict they want. And I will only be able to hope that you do the right thing and return a verdict of 'not guilty.'

"Thank you."

Talon walked back to her seat and sat down next to her client.

"That was," he whispered, "not what I expected."

Talon nodded. "No one did. That's why it might work."

Judge Kozlowski took a moment to let the remnants of Talon's opening dissipate. Then he shook his head slightly to himself and looked down at the prosecution table. "The State may call its first witness."

Cecilia stood up. "May it please the Court, the State calls Karen Burgess to the stand."

CHAPTER 36

Karen Burgess was waiting in the hallway, since she wasn't supposed to listen to the opening statements either. Normally, when there were two prosecutors, the one who wasn't doing the examination would go fetch the witness from the hallway. Cecilia was doing the examination, as indicated by her being the one who formally called the witness, but apparently fetching witnesses was beneath Riordan. He spun his chair and tossed a glance at some prosecution staffer seated in the back row, and in turn, that person stepped outside to bring Karen inside.

In any event, a few moments later, Karen Burgess was sworn in and seated on the witness stand, ready as she could be for the first question from Cecilia Thompson, one of the prosecutors trying to put her son in prison for the rest of his life.

"Could you please state your name for the record?" Cecilia began.

"Karen Burgess."

On the other hand, Cecilia was also one of the prosecutors seeking justice for the murder of Karen's parents. There was an arc family members would often travel when they were related to both the victim and the defendant. The needs of the surviving family member tended to take immediate precedence over the emotions of losing the other family member. It was a function of the urgency of those needs. Hunter got arrested. Hunter got charged. Hunter needed a lawyer. Hunter was looking at life in prison. But Karen's parents? They were beyond help.

As those initial needs were met and the case proceeded at a more or less manageable rate, the family member would start to lose support for the defendant, in part because of guilt for helping the defendant in the first place. It was gradual, and the person usually tried to keep it from other family members who might not be feeling the same conflict. 'It was *my* parents, Chad,' Karen had reminded her husband. It wasn't a question of whether Karen was on that arc. The question was where on it she was. Talon had been trying to judge it, hoping the timing would work out. For the jury, Cecilia's questioning was designed to introduce the victims and explain the dynamics of the major players. For Talon, it was data to know whether Karen was where Talon wanted her on that arc.

"Do you know the defendant, Hunter Burgess?" Cecilia asked, gesturing behind her toward the defense table without actually turning around.

But Karen looked. "Yes."

"How do you know him?"

Karen looked away again and delivered her answer directly to Cecilia. "He's my son."

She wouldn't look at Hunter again during her testimony.

"Did you also know Arnold and Florence Grovequist?" Cecilia continued the cast of characters.

"Yes," Karen answered. She was less emotional than Talon might have expected. She wasn't sure yet whether that was good or bad.

"How did you know them?"

"They're my parents," Karen answered, insisting on using the present tense despite the phrasing of Cecilia's question.

Cecilia knew better than to argue the point with a sympathetic witness, but in a murder case she did have to establish the victims were actually dead.

"Your parents have both passed away, is that correct?" Cecilia phrased it as delicately as she could have.

"Yes," Karen agreed.

"And their deaths are the subject of the case we're all here for today, correct?"

Talon grinned slightly. Cecilia didn't know where Karen was on the arc either. She was tiptoeing.

"Correct," Karen answered,

"And just so the jury understands," Cecilia prefaced the next question, "you didn't personally witness the events that led to their deaths, correct?"

Karen nodded. "Correct."

"Okay, so I won't be asking you any questions about that," Cecilia said.

"Thank you," Karen replied.

She was pretty far along that arc, Talon assessed.

"Instead," Cecilia continued, "could you explain to the jury the living arrangements among you, your husband, your son, and your parents? I believe there are two houses on your property, is that right?"

"Yes, that's right," Karen confirmed.

"Who lived in which house?"

"I live in the main house with my husband, Chad," Karen answered, "and Hunter." She still didn't look at him. "My parents lived in the smaller house farther from the road."

"The lake house?" Cecilia suggested.

"I don't really like to call it that," Karen said. "My husband calls it that, but it's just a regular house. It's smaller than the main house, which was perfect for my parents when they started to need more help getting around."

Definitely far along the arc, Talon concluded.

"You said Hunter lived with you and your husband in the main house," Cecilia said. "Did he also sometimes live at the smaller house with your parents?"

"Honestly?" Karen said. "No, not really. There was an extra room with a day bed in it and sometimes he'd fall asleep there, but I wouldn't say he was living there."

Maybe the end of the arc.

"Oh, okay," Cecilia accepted the answer gladly. "So, would he have had any reason to ever be over there?"

Karen shrugged. "They were his grandparents. He went there sometimes to visit them. Not very often, but sometimes. Especially if I nagged him to do it, or I just needed him out of the house."

Cecilia nodded at the answer. "On the day your parents died, Ms. Burgess, did you nag your son to go visit your parents or otherwise send him to their home?"

Karen shook her head. "No. I don't think I even saw him that day. I have no idea what he was doing." She paused. "Well, maybe I do now. I don't know."

Ouch. Definitely at the end of the arc. That answer stung.

Cecilia knew it too. She couldn't actually ask Karen to speculate on what Hunter was doing that day. But the answer she gave communicated it to the jury anyway. It was the perfect place to end her questioning. "No further questions," she announced.

Judge Kozlowski looked down at Talon. "Any cross-examination, Ms. Winter?"

"Yes, Your Honor."

Talon stepped out from behind her table to conduct her cross but didn't crowd Karen. The jury wouldn't like that. And it wasn't like she was trying to make Karen crack and admit she was the one who really killed her parents. In fact, Talon didn't really have any questions for her, but the jury would expect her to ask at least a few questions of the State's first witness, and she didn't really want to end Karen's testimony on that last comment of hers.

"Hello. Ms. Burgess," Talon started. "I just want to confirm, you were not in your parents' house when what happened happened, correct?"

"Correct," Karen answered.

"You were at your house, the main house, is that it?"

"Yes, that's it, Ms. Winter," Karen answered coldly. Talon was glad the fees were all paid up.

"Were you contacted by the police that night?"

"Yes. They came to the main house to tell us what had happened to my parents," Karen explained, "and to tell us that they had arrested Hunter for murder."

Okay, we don't need to go down that road, Talon thought.

"Do you know how long it was between the time the police arrived and the time they came to your house?"

"Um, I'm not sure," Karen answered. "I mean, long enough to see what happened, and arrest Hunter, and figure out where we lived."

"So, a little while anyway," Talon suggested.

"I suppose so," Karen said.

"They didn't come to your house first, right?" Talon just wanted it to be crystal clear.

"Right."

"Because by the time they got to your house," Talon said,

"they already knew what had happened. So, they must have gone there first."

Karen thought for a moment. "That makes sense."

Of course, it does, Talon thought.

"No further questions."

Cecilia didn't have any redirect-examination and so Karen was finished. Almost.

"May this witness be excused?" Judge Kozlowski asked. It was the question the judge always asked when a witness finished testifying. If they were excused, they could sit and watch the proceedings with their husband. Usually, the answer was a simple 'Yes' from each lawyer. But Talon threw a wrench in that.

"Actually no, Your Honor," she said. "I'd like Ms. Burgess to be subject to recall."

That meant Talon might call Karen as a witness in her case-in-chief. It also meant Karen couldn't watch the trial after all. But she seemed okay with that. When Judge Kozlowski explained she was subject to recall and therefore was still excluded from the proceedings, she just shrugged and said, "That's fine."

Then she walked to the back of the courtroom and exited, without a glance at either her son or her husband.

CHAPTER 37

After Karen Burgess, the State called pretty much every cop who had responded to the scene that night. Most of them didn't have a lot to add, except for the cumulative effect of cop after cop telling the jury they'd never seen anything like that before in, lo, their so many years on the force.

The crime scene was horrendous. There was no argument about that. And since there was no argument about it, there wasn't much cross-examination either. The issues she really cared about — the unlawful entry and the failure to give Hunter a psych eval immediately — had already been litigated, and having lost them, they were irrelevant and therefore inadmissible to the jury. Cross-examining every cop who went inside that bedroom just meant doubling the amount of time they talked about it.

Talon only cared about the first cop they called to the stand, the last one they called, and the one they didn't call at all.

The first one was the veteran, Sergeant Unker. The last one was a newbie deputy named Alicia Yannick. Talon only had a few questions for each of them, but the answers to those questions would outline the edges of that chasm she told the jury about.

Riordan did the direct examination of Unker, standing to

announce the sergeant dramatically, then placing himself near the witness stand. Unker marched into the courtroom, his right hand raised almost before he reached the judge. He took the stand and nodded to Riordan, and they were off.

"Please state your name for the record."

"Michael Unker."

"How are you employed, sir?"

"I am a deputy sheriff with the Pierce County Sheriff's Department."

"How long have you been a deputy sheriff?"

"Almost twenty years."

"What is your current rank?"

"Sergeant."

And so it went, remarkably identical to his testimony at the suppression hearing Talon lost. The only difference was what the lawyers were focusing on. The first time, it was whether Unker had the legal authority to enter the home. The judge having decided that he did, Talon was prohibited from raising the same complaint to the jury. Instead, the focus now was on what Unker saw when he made that questionable entry.

"I observed the defendant standing in the front entryway," Unker answered when Riordan finally got him there, "approximately six feet from the door."

"Please describe how the defendant looked when you saw him," Riordan directed. "And specifically, the condition of his clothing and anything in his hands."

"Right." Unker knew why he was there. "The defendant appeared surprised by our sudden entry. He froze where he was standing and stared at us. I don't recall exactly what he was wearing, but I do recall that it was covered in blood. He also had blood spatter over about half of his face. I remember thinking how wide his eyes were and how much wider they seemed with all of the blood smeared around them. His shoes were especially bloody, and I noticed blood collecting on the floor around him from the drips coming off his clothing."

"Was he holding anything?" Riordan prompted.

"Right. Yes." Unker nodded. "In one hand he was holding a baseball bat. I think it was his left hand. The grip of the bat was in his hand and the end of it was resting on the floor."

"What was the condition of the bat?" Riordan asked. "Was there blood on it also?"

"Oh yeah," Unker almost chuckled. "It was basically all red, and so was his hand that was holding it. There was already a puddle of blood under the tip of it. I remember noticing the blood was so fresh, the bat was glistening."

"Upon seeing the defendant covered in blood and holding a weapon also covered in blood," Riordan continued, "what actions did you take?"

"We immediately restrained the defendant," Unker said. "We had obviously surprised him, and we didn't want to lose that advantage, especially with him holding a weapon. Several of us rushed to him and took him to the ground. He was handcuffed and removed from the home."

"At that point, did you know what had happened yet?" Riordan asked.

Unker shook his head. "No, sir. But I had a pretty good suspicion."

"Was that suspicion confirmed when you went deeper into the house?"

"Yes, sir," Unker answered.

"What was your suspicion," Riordan asked, "and what confirmed it?"

"My suspicion was some sort of extreme violence," Unker answered. "It was confirmed when I went into the bedroom and saw the bloodiest murder scene I've ever seen in my twenty years as a law enforcement officer."

Riordan took that opportunity to show the jury the crime scene photos again. There was a belief in prosecution circles that showing the jury the horror of the crime scene would increase their desire for justice, even revenge. But there had to be a point where the jurors had seen it enough and would start to resent the prosecutor for making them have to look at it so many times. Talon hoped they'd reached that point already, or would soon.

Talon didn't care much about the rest of Riordan's direct examination. She'd heard it all before, and she wasn't contesting that grandma and grandpa had been murdered. She paid enough attention to know when Riordan had finished, then stepped forward to conduct her cross-examination.

"You said my client appeared surprised when you burst into the home?"

"Yes, ma'am," Unker agreed.

"And you and your men immediately tackled him to the ground, is that right?"

"We took him to the ground," Unker tweaked the phrasing slightly. "Yes, ma'am."

Talon didn't care how they phrased it. She only cared about the timing. "Immediately?"

"Yes, ma'am," Unker answered. "Only as long as it took us to assess the situation, and that didn't take but a second or two."

"Because it was so obvious what had happened?" Talon suggested.

"Well, we didn't know the full details in those first few seconds, ma'am," Unker admitted, "but it was clear that he needed to be immediately restrained so we were safe, and so we could search the home for anyone who might need assistance."

"Because you walked in on that and your first instinct was to help, correct?"

"Correct, ma'am," Unker agreed. "My first instinct, and also my job."

Talon didn't need that last part, but she'd take it. "Thank you, sergeant. No further questions."

"Any redirect examination, Mr. Riordan?" Judge Kozlowski asked.

Riordan frowned. He was always ready for a bit more spotlight, but Talon's questions hadn't raised any issues he needed to address. Not yet anyway. "Uh, no, Your Honor. Thank you."

Unker was excused then, and Talon settled in for the coming procession of cops who had no information helpful to her strategy. The challenge would be to look engaged without appearing concerned, all while thinking about the witnesses who would be coming later.

CHAPTER 38

What seemed like three-hundred and seventy-nine cops later, the State finally reached the end of their patrol parade.

"The State calls Deputy Alicia Yannick to the stand," Cecilia announced.

It felt like Cecilia and Riordan had been alternating witnesses, but a closer examination revealed Riordan was doing the ones with valuable information and Cecilia did the rest. Even Karen Burgess hadn't had that much information to provide; she was only there to tell the jury her parents were dead.

Deputy Yannick was summoned into the courtroom by the same prosecutor's office staffer, and she marched toward the judge in full uniform. Judge Kozlowski swore her in and then she sat on the witness stand, leaning forward as if somehow still at attention even while sitting. Talon thought it was both annoying and endearing. She imagined the jury did too.

"Could you please state your name for the record?" Cecilia began.

"Alicia Marie Yannick."

"How are you employed, Ms. Yannick?"

"I'm a deputy with the Pierce County Sheriff's Department."

"So, it's Deputy Yannick?" Cecilia confirmed, although that was how she'd announced her to begin with.

"Yes, ma'am."

"What are your current duties and assignments?" Cecilia moved on.

"I am a patrol deputy in the third quadrant," Yannick answered. "Currently, I work the graveyard shift, midnight to eight a.m."

"Does the third quadrant include Lake Tapps?"

"Yes, ma'am, it does," Yannick confirmed.

"Were your duties and assignments the same at the time of this incident as they are now?" Cecilia asked.

Yannick frowned slightly. "No, ma'am. I was also a patrol deputy then, but I was working swing shift, from four p.m. to midnight."

"Okay, thanks for that clarification," Cecilia said. This was all preliminary stuff anyway. Yannick could have said she was on moon patrol now, so long as she testified that she was the one who was tasked with contacting the residents of the main house.

"Did you have any involvement in the case we are here for now, Deputy Yannick?"

"Yes, ma'am," Yannick answered. "I didn't respond to the initial call, but when it was reported as a homicide—a double homicide—then it was all hands on deck, and I self-dispatched to the incident address."

"Did you go inside the house and see the actual crime scene?" Cecilia asked. If so, she could show the jury those horrendous photographs one more time.

"No, ma'am," Yannick answered.

Thank God, thought Talon. She hoped the jurors felt the same.

"By the time I arrived, the scene was already locked down. So, I worked perimeter and made sure no one went in or out. Well, at my checkpoint anyway."

"Did you have any other duties assigned to you that night?" Cecilia knew.

"Yes, ma'am. After a while."

"And what was that new duty or assignment?"

"Sergeant Unker told me to go to the next house over and contact the residents to see if they might have heard or seen anything prior to the murders."

"And did you do that?"

"I did, ma'am."

"Do you remember who you spoke with at that house?" Cecilia asked.

"Yes, ma'am," Yannick answered. "Normally I might have to check my notes if it was just a neighbor, but it turned out the woman was the daughter of the victims and the mother of the suspect. Her name was Karen Burgess. I remember that. Also, my subpoena said *The State of Washington versus Hunter Burgess*, so I could remember the last name that way too."

Cecilia nodded at that unnecessary extra information. "Did you advise her of the situation?"

"I did, ma'am."

"How did she react?" Cecilia asked.

"Well, at first, I thought she reacted strangely because I thought she was just a neighbor," Yannick answered. "She was extremely distraught. Not that a neighbor couldn't be distraught over a murder, but this was much more than I would have expected. Then she said the victims were her parents, and I understood why she was so upset."

"Did you also advise her that her own son had been arrested

for the murders?" Cecilia asked.

Yannick smiled weakly. "Um, yes, I did. Although I was advised later that I probably shouldn't have done that."

"Why is that?" Cecilia asked, either because she herself was perhaps curious or because the jury definitely was.

"Well, it was an active investigation," Yannick explained the explanation she'd been given, "and she was close to both the victims and the suspect, so she might have done something crazy, I mean unexpected, that could have compromised the early stages of the investigation."

"Did she in fact do anything like that?" Cecilia asked, again because the jury was going to be curious about that. Good prosecutors leave jurors with no questions unanswered, even tangential questions like this one.

"Oh, no, ma'am," Yannick answered. "She just got really sad, it seemed like. She sat down and didn't say anything for the longest time. Then she finally asked if she could go see them."

"What did you tell her?"

"I told her no," Yannick said. "And I found out later that was the right answer. It took several more hours before forensics was done. She could have contaminated the crime scene. Plus, from what I heard, it was pretty bad in that bedroom. I think it would have been really upsetting for her."

"Did you stay with her then?" Cecilia asked.

Yannick tilted her head. "Stay? Oh no. No, I had completed my task, so I returned to the scene to assist further."

"You left Ms. Burgess alone?"

Yannick thought for a moment, clearly wanting to get the answer correct. "Yes, ma'am. After determining her relationship to the case and instructing her not to go to the crime scene, I left her there alone. I told her a detective would likely be coming by, but I didn't know when, and it can take them hours to talk with every possible witness."

Cecilia took a moment to check her notes, then nodded to herself. "Did that conclude your involvement in the case?"

"Yes, ma'am," Yannick frowned. "I wanted to do more, but we'd been out there for a while by then, and I still had reports to write before my shift ended, so they sent me away."

"Thank you, Deputy Yannick," Cecilia said. "No further questions."

"Cross-examination, Ms. Winter?" Judge Kozlowski invited.

"Thank you, Your Honor, yes." Talon came out from behind her counsel table again but this time she did get a little too close to the witness. Yannick was a cop; Talon was supposed to look like she was confronting her. But truthfully, Yannick's testimony had been helpful. Talon just wanted to highlight a few portions.

"How long had you been working the perimeter before Sergeant Unker tasked you to contact the residents of the next house over?"

Yannick thought for a moment. "I'm not sure exactly. I know I had been doing perimeter for a while because I was happy to be given a different task."

"Could it have been an hour?" Talon suggested.

"Oh, easily," Yannick agreed. "Maybe two. Probably not. Probably one."

"One hour?"

"Yeah," Yannick confirmed, "give or take."

"In fact, when you finished that task," Talon reminded her, "they sent you home because you had already been there so long. Isn't that right?"

Yannick nodded. "That is right. I mean, I was up there with Ms. Burgess for a while, you know, until she seemed like she was going to be okay, but I see your point. I was there a while, but I can't say exactly how long."

Talon wished she were surprised. "That's fine, deputy. You did your best. That's what we're all trying to do. No further questions."

"Any redirect-examination?" the judge inquired of Cecilia as Talon returned to her seat.

"No, Your Honor," Cecilia confirmed.

"May the witness be excused?" Kozlowski asked.

"Yes, Your Honor," Cecilia answered.

"Sure," Talon put in, before remembering to add, "Your Honor."

It had been a long day. A long week, in fact. Cops were the most boring witnesses ever. They always showed up in full uniform, complete with stick up ass. It was all 'Yes, ma'am' and 'No, sir' and it took forever, even though most of them didn't do even as much as Deputy Yannick.

The good news was that the State was almost finished with their case-in-chief. The bad news was that their last witness was the medical examiner, and his testimony was going to be gruesome.

CHAPTER 39

The only cop the State didn't call was the only one Talon had been hoping for: the lead detective, Scott Tomlinson. In truth, lead detectives usually didn't do anything themselves; they directed others to do things, then collected the results. The case wasn't a whodunit where the detective could unravel the investigation for the jury. The first cop in the door tackled the defendant within three seconds. Everything else was cleanup. That might have been why the State didn't bother calling Tomlinson. But it didn't give Talon anyone to cross-examine about the things they didn't do in their investigation. That was probably the real reason they didn't call him.

Talon would just have to make do with the medical examiner then.

"As its last witness, the State calls Dr. Sanjay Randhawa," Riordan announced. Of course, it was Riordan. He wasn't going to let Cecilia handle the autopsy testimony.

Dr. Randhawa was brought into the courtroom and made his way slowly to the judge to be sworn in. He was in his late 50s, skinny, with graying temples and thick eyebrows over wire-framed glasses. He took the stand and looked almost blankly at Riordan, as if he was willing to be there, but not especially happy about it.

"Hello, doctor," Riordan began. "Could you please state your name for the record?"

"Sanjay Randhawa," came the reply.

"How are you employed, sir?"

"I'm an assistant medical examiner with the Pierce County Medical Examiner's Office."

"Do you need to be a medical doctor to hold that position?" Riordan asked.

"Yes, definitely," Randhawa answered. "You have to have a bachelor's degree, preferably in biology or a similar science, then a medical degree, then a residency in pathology, often followed by another residency in forensic pathology."

"And you have all that?" Riordan said.

"Yes," Randhawa answered, seemingly bored with his own accomplishments. "I have all that."

"Is conducting autopsies one of your duties at the medical examiner's office?" Riordan moved along.

"I would say that is almost my only duty," Randhawa answered. "That's what an assistant medical examiner does."

"Of course, it is," Riordan replied. He didn't want the jury to think he didn't know everything already. "Let's talk about the autopsy in this case. Did you conduct the autopsies of Arnold Grovequist and Florence Grovequist?"

Dr. Randhawa nodded. "I did."

"And were you able to determine a cause and manner of death from those autopsies?"

"I was."

"What was the cause and manner of death for Arnold Grovequist?" Riordan asked first.

"The cause of death was blunt force trauma," Randhawa answered. "The manner of death was homicide."

"And what was the cause of death for Florence Grovequist?"

"Also blunt force trauma and homicide," Randhawa confirmed.

Riordan was really dragging it out.

"Could you explain to the jury," Riordan directed, "what is meant by the term 'blunt force trauma'?"

Dr. Randhawa turned to the jurors. "The best way to think of it is in opposition to what we call sharp force trauma," he explained. "Sharp force trauma is what happens when you cut or stab someone with something sharp, like a knife. The skin is lacerated, and the interior of the body is opened up. In contrast, with blunt force trauma, the skin generally is not broken, although that can also happen, but the primary source of injury is from the force of a non-sharp, or blunt, object traveling through the skin into the interior of the body, causing damage from the resultant shock wave. Sharp force trauma cuts and divides parts of the body. Blunt force trauma crushes them."

"How can blunt force trauma lead to death, doctor?" Riordan prompted.

Randhawa looked at Riordan as he posed the obviously rehearsed question, then turned back to the jury box. "The two main ways blunt force trauma can cause death are through organ failure and internal hemorrhaging."

"And why is that?" Riordan encouraged.

"Well, as I said, blunt force is a crushing force," Randhawa explained. "If an organ is crushed enough, it can rupture, leading to failure. Bones can also break and then lacerate nearby organs. So, if your liver ruptures, or your kidneys, or really any organ, that alone can be fatal if untreated. In addition, veins and arteries can also rupture, leading to internal bleeding which prevents organs from receiving the oxygen they need to survive. Also, the buildup of blood from internal bleeding can create additional force on organs causing them to fail. There is also the risk of sepsis if waste enters the interior of the body through the rupture of say, the large intestine."

"So, it sounds like blunt force trauma can be really bad," Riordan summed up weirdly.

Randhawa frowned slightly. "Yes, it is bad."

"Is it even worse if it's to the head?" Riordan encouraged.

"I wouldn't say it's worse," Randhawa answered, "but the brain is peculiarly susceptible to blunt force trauma."

"Why is that?" Riordan asked.

"Well, for one thing," Randhawa turned again to the jurors, "the brain is actually very well shielded from sharp force trauma. The skull is very thick. It would take a very sharp object with a large amount of force to split the skull. Such a blow would be far more likely to cause life-threatening injuries because of the resultant blunt force traveling to the brain than from whatever blade struck the outside of the skull."

"How would that happen?" Riordan kept the prompts coming. No wonder he got paid the big bucks.

"The force of the blow would travel through the skull and cause blood vessels in the brain to rupture," Randhawa answered. "Our brains have become so large that they completely fill up the inside of our skulls. There's no room for blood to be in there, but there's also no way for the blood to drain out, so it will start to pool and put pressure against the brain. If enough blood collects, it will start to crush the brain, leading to even more bleeding and more crushing of the brain tissue until eventually death ensues."

"Did all of that happen in these cases?" Riordan asked.

"Every type of blunt force trauma I've described?" Dr. Randhawa clarified. "And every possible resultant injury?"

Riordan shrugged. "Sure."

Randhawa thought for a moment, then nodded. "Actually yes. The bodies suffered blunt force trauma over almost every part of the body, and especially to the head and torso. The brains were damaged more than enough to cause death, but there were also potentially fatal injuries to all of the major organs in both subjects."

"Did the victims' advanced age play any role in their deaths?" Riordan followed up.

Dr. Randhawa frowned for a moment in thought. "Certainly, it would have made it easier for the blunt force to cause injury. With advanced age, bones become brittle and soft tissue is more easily torn. But honestly, given the sheer number of injuries and the apparent force used to inflict them, I don't think anyone would have been able to survive what happened to these two people."

Riordan seemed to like that answer. He smiled and nodded, then looked up to the judge. "No further questions."

Judge Kozlowski nodded down to Talon. "Cross-examination?"

"Yes, Your Honor," Talon confirmed. She had a few questions for him in his role as the doctor who performed the autopsy, plus a few for his role as the State's final witness.

"Hello, doctor," she started.

"Hello," he responded.

So far, so good.

"Blunt force trauma can be inflicted either with a weapon or just with the body, correct?" Talon asked. "Fists, feet, elbows can all cause blunt force trauma as well, correct?"

"Correct," Randhawa confirmed. "In fact, that's probably

the most common way to inflict blunt force trauma. Just a punch or a kick. I think we've probably all experienced that to one degree or another."

"But not to the degree experienced in this case?" Talon was quick to follow up.

"Oh no," Randhawa agreed. "This case was extreme."

"You can't cause this extensive of injuries using only your fist or feet, right?"

Randhawa shook his head. "No. These were caused by a weapon. I believe the police recovered a baseball bat, which is consistent with the injuries on this case."

"But still, you could kill someone using only your fists, right?"

Randhawa nodded. "Oh yes. I have definitely seen cases where a person suffered fatal injuries just from punches or kicks."

"And it would be easier to injure someone with just a punch if the victim was elderly, right?" Talon asked.

"Yes," Randhawa agreed. "As I said before, less force would be required to inflict the injuries where bones and soft tissue are older and more brittle."

Talon stepped aside and pointed to her client. "A person my client's size and age, he could inflict fatal injuries on two old people with the use of a baseball bat, correct?"

Randhawa narrowed his eyes at Talon. "Are you asking me whether I think your client could have killed the victims in this case?"

"I'm asking whether he would have needed a baseball bat to do it."

Randhawa frowned again. "I agree he wouldn't have needed one, but that is definitely what was used in this case."

That was the best possible answer. Talon would have loved

to walk off on that response, but there was the little matter of not having anyone else to ask about why the cops didn't do the thing she wanted the jury to think they should have done.

"When a body is transported to the morgue for an autopsy," Talon began the setup for her final question, "what happens to the clothes?"

"We examine the clothes for any evidence that might be related to the purposes of the autopsy," Randhawa answered. "For example, gunshot residue or tears from a knife. We document that examination in writing and with photographs. Then the clothing is removed and collected to be handed over to the police."

"So, in this case, you gave the clothing to the police?"

"Yes," Randhawa confirmed.

"And that clothing was pretty bloody, wasn't it?"

"It was bloody, yes," Randhawa agreed.

"Very bloody, right?" Talon suggested. "Like, literally dripping in blood, correct?"

"There was a lot of blood," Randhawa allowed. "Yes."

"More than enough to get a DNA sample, right?" Talon said. "Do you know why the police never sent it out for DNA testing?"

That brought Riordan to his feet. "Objection!"

The exact reaction Talon wanted. 'Objection' was lawyer-talk for 'Ouch!'

"Calls for speculation," Riordan provided the basis for his objection. "This witness can't speak to what another witness did or why."

"Well, I actually asked him about what another *non*-witness did *not* do," Talon responded up to Judge Kozlowski. "And since Mr. Riordan kind of announced that this would be their last witness, I thought I should bring it up finally."

Judge Kozlowski took a moment before responding,

presumably to filter out what he wanted to say from what he could say; the jury was there and very much listening to what the ruling would be. Talon hoped they were also looking at Riordan because he was bending over and having an intense whispered conversation with his co-counsel. When he finished and stood up straight again, Kozlowski asked him, "Anything to add, Mr. Riordan?"

"Yes, Your Honor," Riordan answered. "To the extent I may have said Dr. Randhawa was the State's last witness, I may have misspoken. The State will also be calling Detective Tomlinson."

"Ah," Judge Kozlowski replied with a slight lift of his chin.

"We may need a brief recess," Riordan continued, "to, um, confirm he's here."

To call him and tell him to hightail it to the court, Talon knew, *and grab a jacket on the way out the door.*

Kozlowski looked over to Talon. "Ms. Winter?"

"Based on that, Your Honor, I'll withdraw the question," Talon said. "I'd rather hear the detective try to answer it anyway."

CHAPTER 40

It took a little over two hours for Tomlinson to arrive. Probably his day off, Talon figured. He had managed to put on a coat but apparently couldn't find a tie. He seemed a little out of breath, and he could have used a haircut, but Talon suspected that might be his usual look. He had not shaven. Definitely his day off.

After a brief whispered huddle with the prosecutors, Tomlinson took a seat in the front row of the gallery and Riordan informed the bailiff they were ready. Kozlowski wasted no time taking the bench and it only took a minute for the jury to reassemble in the jury box so Riordan could announce, "The State calls Scott Tomlinson to the stand."

Yeah, we all knew that, Talon thought as Tomlinson stood up and approached the witness stand to be sworn in.

Riordan did the examination again, of course. Tomlinson was such an important witness that they had tried to hide him from the jury. That had to have been Riordan's decision. Now that his own decision had backfired, it only made sense that he should also screw up the examination.

It was all the usual preliminary stuff. Scott Tomlinson. Detective with the Pierce County Sheriff's Department. Been a detective for 100 years. Been a cop for 200 years before that. So amazingly awesome was promoted to detective before he was even born. Made absolutely no mistakes ever and certainly not in this case.

"As the lead detective, what was your main role in this case?" Riordan finally asked.

"My main role was collecting the evidence into a central location and passing it on to the prosecutor's office," Tomlinson answered.

"Is part of that also deciding what evidence to seek and collect in the first place?" Riordan asked.

Tomlinson hesitated. "I suppose so."

"Well, for example, in this case," Riordan asked, "did you order any firearm testing?"

Tomlinson frowned at him. "Um, no."

"Why not?"

"Because there was no firearm involved."

Duh.

"But if there had been a firearm involved," Riordan continued, "you would have been the one to order test firing to, say, link bullets from the crime scene with the suspected murder weapon, correct?"

"Yes," Tomlinson agreed. "I would order that kind of testing if I needed to link a particular firearm with bullets or casings found at the crime scene."

"Did you order any such testing on the weapon in this case?" Riordan asked.

Tomlinson raised an eyebrow. "The baseball bat?"

"Yes."

"No," Tomlinson answered. "I did not do that."

"Why not?" Riordan was firing off each question almost

before Tomlinson had answered the last.

"Because there's no such test," Tomlinson said. "There's no test to connect a baseball bat to a crime scene. And anyway, the defendant was holding the bat when he was apprehended, so we didn't really need a test."

"A-ha!" Riordan jabbed a finger in the air. "And that is exactly my point. You didn't need to do any sort of ballistic testing in this case because the murder weapon was literally still in the hands of the murderer."

"Right," Tomlinson agreed.

"Likewise," Riordan continued, "did you order a photomontage or a lineup to confirm the defendant was the person your deputies found inside the house?"

"Um, no."

"Why not?"

"Because photomontages and lineups are for when a person gets away, and you need witnesses to identify a potential suspect later," Tomlinson explained. "Here, we arrested him ourselves, inside the home. I don't even know who we would show a photomontage to."

"Right, right," Riordan seemed very impressed with himself. "Did you order fingerprints be taken off the bat to see if the defendant had touched it?"

Again, a pause from the witness. "No."

"Why not?"

"Because it was in his hand when he was arrested," Tomlinson answered. "We don't need additional testing to confirm what we observed ourselves."

Riordan nodded along to the answer. "Exactly. And is that also why you didn't order DNA testing of the blood on the baseball bat? Because it was already clear that the blood was from the bodies beaten to death inside the same home?"

"Yes." Tomlinson nodded. "It wasn't like we conducted a traffic stop on some random person and found a bloody baseball bat in the trunk. We weren't looking for the victims, and we didn't need to connect the defendant with the crime scene. He was literally found there with the weapon in his hand."

Riordan smiled, in Tomlinson's direction, but mostly at himself. "I think that explains it. Thank you, Detective Tomlinson. No further questions."

Talon stood up even as the judge invited her with, "Any cross-examination, Ms. Winter?"

"Thanks for coming to court, detective," she began. "You didn't expect to testify today, did you?"

Tomlinson offered a sheepish smile and a boy scout salute. "Always prepared."

"If you say so," Talon responded. "Let's talk about that DNA testing you didn't order. That would be your decision whether to order it, correct?"

"Yes, that was my decision," Tomlinson confirmed.

"If I understood your testimony," Talon said, "you didn't order any DNA testing because you kind of knew the blood was the victims', is that right?"

"Yes, there was no need," Tomlinson insisted.

Talon nodded in response. She waited a few moments before asking her next question, using the awkwardness of the silence to draw everyone back in and make sure they were paying attention. "What about suspect DNA?"

Tomlinson's confident expression faltered. "Suspect DNA?"

"Yes. DNA from the suspect. Isn't it possible, even common, for suspects to be injured during their attacks and also leave blood and therefore DNA behind?"

"I mean, um," Tomlinson shifted in his seat, "I'm not sure if it's common, but it can happen. Usually, it's more when the weapon is bladed and there's a struggle, which isn't what happened here."

"So, you're telling this jury," Talon posed, "that there was no chance at all that the person who committed this incredibly violent, seemingly out of control attack might have also injured themselves and left behind some blood to confirm their presence at the crime scene?"

"I think it's highly unlikely, counsel," Tomlinson dug in.

"But not impossible, correct?"

Tomlinson hesitated, but there was only one truthful answer. "I can't say it's impossible, just very, very unlikely."

"What happened to being prepared?" Talon teased. "Wouldn't it be better to know that for sure?"

"There are dozens, even hundreds of decisions that need to be made in every case," Tomlinson defended. "It didn't make sense to order DNA testing."

"Because you already had your suspect?"

"Yes."

"And it had to be him who did it?"

"Yes."

"Unless he didn't," Talon said. "But you didn't want to look into that possibility, I guess."

Before Tomlinson could address Talon's non-question, she posed another. "Please tell the jury what a mixed DNA sample is. If you know," she goaded.

"Of course, I know," Tomlinson told her. Then he turned to the jury to explain. "A mixed sample is when you find both victim DNA and suspect DNA at the same location."

"Which would indicate the suspect and the victim were bleeding at the same time, presumably from the violence of the attack," Talon added. "Can you think of any better evidence to show a person committed the crime?"

Tomlinson frowned. "I don't know. Maybe a cop walking in and witnessing the crime firsthand."

"Oh, right, that would be awesome," Talon agreed with several exaggerated nods. Then she stopped and pointed at Tomlinson. "But you don't actually have that in this case either, do you?"

Tomlinson hesitated.

"I mean, the cops walked in on my client being in the house," Talon agreed, "but they didn't actually observe the crime, did they?"

"Well, it was immediately after the crime," Tomlinson defended.

"Was it?"

Tomlinson took a moment. "Yes."

"Hm," Talon responded. She could get into an argument with Tomlinson then or explain to the jury later why he was at least potentially wrong. Easy choice. "One more question then, detective."

"Okay," Tomlinson braced himself.

"Who inherited from the victims' wills?" she asked. "If you know. I mean, it's potential motive, so you should know, but maybe you don't."

"We did look into that," Tomlinson was happy to answer. "But there was nothing special about their estate planning. It was a typical mix of life insurance and bequests. Their daughter Karen was their only child, and the defendant was their only grandkid. Most of it went to her, but the defendant was supposed to get some too. I don't recall the exact amount, but they weren't millionaires, so it wasn't that much. Ten or twenty thousand maybe."

"Nothing to murder someone over?" Talon suggested.

Tomlinson shrugged. "Honestly, I don't think there's ever a reason to murder someone. That's why I do what I do. These were especially senseless murders, so I can't say what your client's motive may have been."

Again, Talon chose to delay that argument to her closing argument. There was just one more thing she needed Tomlinson to say. "Under the law," she asked, "a murderer can't collect an inheritance from his victim, isn't that right?"

Tomlinson nodded. "I believe that's correct."

That was all Talon needed. "Thank you, detective. No further questions."

"Any redirect examination, Mr. Riordan?" the judge inquired.

"Yes, Your Honor," Riordan replied, standing and buttoning his suit coat.

He strode right up to the witness stand. "How long have you been a law enforcement officer again?"

"Twenty-two years."

"How long have you been a detective?"

"Thirteen years."

"How long have you been handling homicide cases?"

"Seven years."

"And in your carefully considered, experienced, dare I say expert, opinion," Riordan blatantly led his witness, "there was no reason to order DNA testing given the unique and peculiar facts of this case, correct?"

"That is correct."

"Has anything the defense attorney said or asked here today changed your opinion that it would have been a waste of time and resources to order DNA testing in this case?"

"Absolutely not, sir."

"Thank you. No further questions."

Riordan sat down again, and Kozlowski invited Talon, "Recross examination?"

"Just one question," Talon assured the judge. She stepped out from behind the counsel table and approached Tomlinson.

First, she reminded him, "You've sworn an oath to tell the truth, detective."

"I know that, counsel," Tomlinson acknowledged with a sneer.

"Okay, good," Talon accepted his response. "So, now that I've asked you what I've asked you, and you've tried to explain it as best you could to this jury, can you honestly say that you don't wish you had ordered that DNA test after all, even if just to shut me up?"

Tomlinson hesitated.

"You swore to tell the truth," Talon repeated. "Looking back now, you kind of wish you'd ordered that DNA test, don't you?"

Further hesitation from Tomlinson, and a frown. He was already answering her question.

"Honestly?" Talon prompted.

Finally, Tomlinson sighed and nodded. "Yes, now that you've made such a big deal about it, I kind of wish I had gone ahead and ordered it so this wouldn't be an issue."

Talon smiled. "But it is an issue," she repeated his word to make sure the jury heard it. "Thank you. No further questions."

Riordan seemed to be considering trying re-redirect examination, but he took a look at Talon and her eager expression and declined. Instead, he allowed Tomlinson to be excused, then announced, as dramatically as the three words would allow, "The State rests."

CHAPTER 41

"Yes!" Talon fist-pumped in the hallway as soon as she got outside the courtroom. She'd managed to get the State's case-in-chief to end on the lead detective admitting there was an 'issue' with their case. The judge adjourned early again, to allow Talon to start her own case-in-chief first thing in the morning. That was standard procedure, but it meant she had earned a half-day to catch her breath and bask in her own awesomeness before returning to the battle.

But the universe had other plans.

A few of them, as it would turn out.

"Trial going well?" It was Cassandra Sondheim, standing outside the courtroom, arms crossed and foot tapping. "Is that why you've been too busy to return my calls?"

Talon wasn't about to feel bad about not returning the calls of a law firm that wanted to use her as a racist prop. But she also wasn't ready to let them off the hook yet either.

"Exactly," Talon answered. "You're a lawyer. You get it. Trial, am I right?"

Talon knew Cassandra did not, in fact, get it. She was a lawyer, but she wasn't a trial lawyer. She was a corporate desk jockey. But Talon also knew she wouldn't want to admit that.

"Oh, totally. Yeah, of course," Cassandra replied. "But also, you know, we kind of need to know what's going on, or if we maybe need to go in a new direction, or what, you know?"

Talon nodded profusely. "Absolutely. That makes complete sense."

Cassandra waited for more, but then sighed and asked, "So, when should I expect to hear from you? Is your trial almost over?"

"It is," Talon confirmed. "Just another witness or two. Then closings, of course. And deliberations. Then the verdict, finally. So, yeah, almost done."

Cassandra forced a tight smile. "So, how long?"

Talon narrowed her eyes. "Hard to say, you know? A week, maybe? Maybe two."

Cassandra took in a sharp breath. "I don't know if we can wait two weeks, Talon."

Talon framed her Native features with her hands. "You want this to be the face of your Tacoma litigation department, don't you?"

"Yes," Cassandra admitted. "Yes, we do."

"Great." Talon patted her on the shoulder as she stepped past her to leave. "I'll call you in a week. Maybe two."

Cassandra called out after her, something about one week being better than two, but Talon was already on to her next task. Cassandra had completely destroyed her post-court high. The bask was over. So, she might as well do the other couple things she didn't want to do.

* * *

Talon knocked on the frame of the open door.

Curt looked up from his computer. "Talon! Oh, um, hi. What's up? How's the trial going?"

Talon stepped in and sat down across his desk from him. She knew she didn't need an invitation.

"Trial's going great," Talon reported. "Well, about as well as could be expected given the whole 'my client is guilty' thing."

"Yeah, that's kind of a recurring problem in our line of work," Curt said. Then he corrected himself, "Your line of work, I mean. I'm just support."

"You're more than support, Curt," Talon assured him.

He just shrugged in reply.

"Look, about that text I sent you the other night," Talon started.

But Curt raised a hand. "We don't need to talk about that. I know that was support too. Been there, done that, right? Not that I don't appreciate the offer, but you know…"

Talon nodded. "I know." And she appreciated not having to talk about it after all. Sometimes the air could be cleared by offering to talk about it, without actually having to talk about it. It was the thought that counted, right?

"Anyway, my case-in-chief starts tomorrow," she changed the subject, "so I need some help confirming the witnesses and making sure they show up at the right place at the right time. Can you do that for me?"

"So, support?" Curt teased.

Talon grimaced. "Yeah, I guess so."

"Happy to do it," Curt said. "Who, when, and where?"

"Where is the hallway right outside Kozlowski's courtroom," Talon said. "Who is Jankles and Hunter's mom. When is nine a.m. sharp for Jankles, and let's say eleven for Karen. We might not even get to her before lunch, but I want her available in case Jankles goes quicker than I expect. Tell her to bring a book to read while she waits."

"On it." Curt gave her a little salute. "What will you be doing?"

Talon sighed. "I need to go talk to Hunter one more time. He needs to know what's coming tomorrow."

* * *

"Ms. Winter," Hunter greeted her as he entered the jail conference room. "I didn't expect to see you today. You said you'd see me tomorrow before the guards took me out of the courtroom."

"I'll see you tomorrow, too," Talon responded.

"I suppose that's true," Hunter agreed. He sat down opposite her. "So why are you here now? Have you changed your mind about me testifying?"

"Oh, no," Talon answered. "Absolutely not. Nothing has changed. I was right about that before the trial started, and I'm still right about that."

"So, why are you here then?" Hunter asked again.

"I wanted to let you know that your mom is going to testify again tomorrow," Talon explained, "and you may not like how it goes."

"Will it help me win the case?" Hunter asked.

Talon nodded. "Well, that's the intent. I wouldn't call her if I thought it would hurt the case."

"Then why wouldn't I like how it goes?" Hunter asked. "If it will help me literally get away with murder."

"Well, because she's your mother," Talon explained, "and I'm not going to be gentle."

"Don't worry, Ms. Winter," Hunter laughed. "You saw what I did to my grandparents. I wasn't gentle either."

CHAPTER 42

"The defense calls Dr. Lawrence Jankles to the stand," Talon announced the next morning after everyone was assembled again, and the judge invited her to begin her case-in-chief.

Curt was there that morning—support—and so fetched Jankles from the hallway upon Talon's announcement. Jankles was dressed in that new suit the upfront fee had paid for, and Talon was glad for it. It was professional without looking expensive, and it was assuredly more tailored than whatever suit jacket he'd been digging out of the back of his closet for the last several years. He carried a new-looking leather briefcase in his left hand too.

Talon had to direct him to step forward to the judge to be sworn in. It betrayed that he hadn't testified very much, at least not recently, but Talon could only hope the jurors wouldn't know that. Jankles swore to tell the truth, the whole truth, and nothing but the truth, then sat down on the witness stand and looked eagerly to Talon. He didn't seem nervous at all. In fact, he seemed almost giddy. She hoped that wouldn't be a bad thing.

"Could you please state your name for the record?" Talon began.

"Larr—Uh, Lawrence Jankles," he managed to answer correctly. "Dr. Lawrence Jankles."

"Doctor," Talon repeated. "Okay, let's talk about that. How are you employed, Dr. Jankles?"

"I am an independent consultant in the field of forensic psychology."

Talon had to admit that sounded impressive. "Do you have specialized education and experience to be able to do that job?"

"Yes, I do," Jankles turned and delivered his answer to the jurors directly. That was good testifying. Maybe he had done this more than Talon realized.

"Could you please explain that education and experience to the jury?" she instructed.

"Absolutely," Jankles replied. Again, he spoke directly to the jury and listed his education, degrees, and years working in the field of psychology. He even explained how the Psy.D. was the less common of the psychology doctorates and intimated, without quite asserting, that it was therefore the more exclusive and superior degree.

"As a consultant in the area of forensic psychology," Talon continued, "do you work directly with patients or review the work of other psychologists?"

"I do both," Jankles answered. "I will always spend some time with the client, but I am often required to review previous work by previous therapists in order to form an accurate diagnosis."

"Did you have occasion," it was time for Talon to move from the general to the specific, "to conduct a forensic psychological examination of my client, Mr. Hunter Burgess, as it relates to this case?"

Jankles nodded. "I did."

"Did your examination include a one-on-one interview of Mr. Burgess?"

"It did."

"And in addition to that examination," Talon continued the setup for Jankles's opinion, "did you review any other materials relevant to Mr. Burgess or this case?"

"Yes," Jankles told the jurors. "I reviewed the police reports and also conducted an inventory of any family history of mental health concerns."

The phrasing of that last part sounded a lot better than 'his lawyer said his mom said her uncle might have been crazy, but also maybe not and didn't want to talk about it'.

"Based on all of that," Talon asked, "were you able to form an opinion regarding Mr. Burgess's behavior upon being contacted by the police?"

"Yes, I was."

"And what was that opinion?"

Jankles turned once again to deliver his diagnosis directly to the people who would be making the decision. "At the time he was contacted by law enforcement, Hunter Burgess was suffering from Acute Stress Disorder." He reached into his briefcase and extracted a two-inch thick softcover book. "Acute Stress Disorder is a specific and recognized trauma- and stressor-related mental disorder, listed in the Diagnostic and Statistical Manual of Mental Disorders, Fifth Edition—what we in the field call the 'DSM-5'—published by the American Psychiatric Association."

"It's called Acute Stress Disorder?" Talon questioned. She knew that sounded pretty vague.

"Yes," Jankles answered. "That particular diagnosis may almost sound like a generalized description of a person's mental state, but it's actually the name for a specific diagnosis, as specific as Schizotypal Personality Disorder or Dissociative Identity Disorder."

"Okay," Talon gladly accepted that answer. "What are the

criteria to reach a diagnosis of Acute Stress Disorder?"

Jankles opened up the DSM-5 to a dog-eared page. Talon hoped he looked like an expert consulting a trusted source, rather than a charlatan reading from a script hidden between the pages.

"The first criteria," Jankles looked up from the book to explain, "is exposure to an actual or threatened death, serious injury, or sexual assault, either by experiencing it themselves, witnessing it directly, or learning that the event happened to a close family member or friend."

Talon nodded. That seemed to fit. "What's the next criteria?"

"The next criteria," Jankles continued, "is experiencing any nine of the following fourteen symptoms: recurrent distressing memories, recurrent distressing dreams, dissociative reactions such as flashbacks, intense or prolonged psychological distress, inability to experience positive emotions, altered sense of reality, inability to remember details of the traumatic event, efforts to avoid memories of the traumatic event, efforts to avoid reminders of the traumatic event, sleep disturbances, irritable or angry behavior, hypervigilance, problems concentrating, and an exaggerated startle response."

"Okay." Talon tried to follow along with the lengthy list. "Did you observe any of those symptoms in Mr. Burgess?"

"Yes."

"Which ones?"

"Well, all of them, really," Jankles said. "But the ones that I think were the quickest to manifest and explain why he acted the way he did when the police contacted him are dissociative reaction, altered sense of reality, and efforts to avoid memories or reminders of the event."

"Doctor," Talon said, "I think people have an idea of how they think they would react if they were to find themselves in a situation like this, that is, a close relative murdered and the police bursting through the door. But people don't always really react the way we think they would or should, do they?"

"No, they don't," Jankles agreed. "In fact," he laid a hand on the book in front of him, "that's sort of the entire point of specialized psychological diagnoses. They explain how a behavior that might seem aberrant is, in fact, perfectly normal."

"Or how a behavior that might seem guilty," Talon suggested, "is actually perfectly consistent with innocence."

"Exactly," Jankles agreed.

"So, let me ask it very specifically then," Talon set it up. "Given your expert diagnosis that Hunter was suffering from Acute Stress Disorder at the time he was confronted by the police, were his actions and behaviors consistent with someone who had, in fact, *not* committed the murders, but rather with an innocent person who had just himself stumbled across the murdered bodies of his own grandparents?"

Jankles nodded along to Talon's question, then turned to the jurors. "Absolutely."

That, thought Talon, *could not have gone better.* "No further questions," she told the judge.

But she and Dr. Jankles weren't out of the woods yet. "Any cross-examination?" the judge asked the prosecutors.

"Oh, definitely," Riordan stood up and rushed around his counsel table. Cecilia had turned into little more than decoration this last part of the trial. Talon wondered whether, since Riordan had done the opening statement, Cecilia might do the closing argument. But she didn't wonder very much.

"Good morning, Mr. Jankles," Riordan started out.

"Doctor Jankles," he corrected.

"Because of your—what did you call it?—a Psy.D.?" Riordan

asked.

"Because of my doctorate, yes," Jankles said.

Riordan rolled his eyes. "Okay. But so the jury understands, you aren't a medical doctor or psychiatrist, correct?"

"Psychiatrists are medical doctors," Jankles pointed out, "and no, I do not have a medical degree."

"But you still hold yourself out as a consultant on psychiatric matters?"

"I am a consultant in the area of forensic psychology," Jankles repeated. "I never said 'psychiatry'."

So far, so good, Talon thought. Jankles was keeping his cool. It was Riordan who was being off-putting.

"Po-tay-to, po-tah-to," Riordan responded. "But fine, let's move on. Your diagnosis of—what did you call it again?—Stressed Out Disorder?"

"Acute Stress Disorder," Jankles corrected him.

Riordan pointed at him. "Yes, that. That's a real diagnosis in the DSM-5, is it?"

"It is," Jankles assured him. "It starts on page two-hundred and eighty."

"Okay, great" Riordan said, stepping back over to his table. "I happen to have my own copy of the DSM-5 here today, so let's take a look at that diagnosis together, shall we?"

Uh-oh, thought Talon.

But Jankles was calm. "Okay."

Riordan walked back to his position directly in front of the witness stand, holding his open copy of the DSM-5 in one hand. "When you explained the diagnosis to the jury, you left off a few of the diagnostic criteria, didn't you, doc?"

Double uh-oh, Talon thought. *That didn't sound good.*

"Are you referring to criteria C, D, and E?" Jankles asked.

"Precisely," Riordan almost shouted.

"Yes, those are present as well," Jankles said.

Riordan frowned. "Are they though, doctor? And if they were, why didn't you tell the jury that before?"

"They are," Jankles assured him, and the jurors, "and the reason I didn't mention them before is because they relate to the patient's status significantly after the event, while Ms. Winter's questions were focused on her client's mental condition immediately afterward."

Riordan hesitated. He looked down at his book again. "Is that so?"

"Yes," Jankles answered. "Criteria C indicates the fourteen symptoms I mentioned must last for at least three days and up to a month, which they did in this case. Criteria D indicates that the disorder results in significant distress or impairment in other areas of the patient's life—for example, being charged with murder. And Criteria E indicates the symptoms were not caused by drug use, and I don't believe you or your officers ever suspected or tested Mr. Burgess for drugs, isn't that right?"

"Um, that is right," Riordan conceded.

"So, all of the criteria are met," Jankles said. "Thank you for clarifying that, sir."

Riordan frowned for a few seconds, then slapped the book shut and returned it to his counsel table, a bit too loudly. Cecilia couldn't quite suppress a flinch.

"You said the defendant's reactions to the police officers were consistent with innocence, that is, with him just coincidentally being in the house and discovering his murdered grandparents," Riordan tried to correct course. "Is that right?"

"That's right," Jankles said.

"But couldn't those same behaviors be consistent with

guilt?" Riordan challenged. "With having just murdered his grandparents and being unexpectedly discovered before he had a chance to get away?"

Jankles thought for a moment. Talon wanted him to say no, but he said something better.

"Yes," Jankles admitted. "His behavior could have been consistent with guilt as well."

Riordan threw his hands up. "Well, if it could be either, what's the difference then?"

"The difference is," Jankles reminded him, Talon, and most importantly, the jurors, "he doesn't have to prove he's innocent. You have to prove he's guilty."

There were a few things you learned along the way as a trial attorney. If you were lucky, you learned them from older, more experienced attorneys telling war stories and not from personal experience. One of those things was never to ask one question too many. Riordan had just made that mistake. The other was knowing when to stop digging and sit down. Riordan, perhaps after forgetting the other rule, remembered that one.

"No further questions," he practically conceded, and trudged back to his seat.

There was no way Talon was going to step on Jankles's exit line with any further Q&A, so she turned down Judge Kozlowski's invitation for redirect examination and let Dr. Larry be excused. He had more than earned that new suit.

"You may call your next witness, Ms. Winter," Judge Kozlowski said.

Talon turned toward the courtroom door, Karen Burgess seated just outside. Then she turned back to the judge. "About that. Could I have a brief recess?"

CHAPTER 43

Judge Kozlowski wasn't thrilled by the request to slow down the trial even further. Riordan actually objected, although he didn't really have any grounds for it. Kozlowski ignored Riordan and instead simply asked Talon, "Do you truly need a recess at this juncture, counsel?"

Talon assured him that she did, but only briefly, and that was enough for the judge to declare a fifteen-minute recess. Some of the jurors probably needed to pee anyway, although the judge didn't say that last part on the record.

Once the jurors were behind the closed jury room door, Talon left Hunter without explanation, told Chad to stay where he was, and hurried into the hallway. She had a hunch, and she needed to confirm it.

Karen Burgess was still in the hallway, although she wasn't sitting. She was standing to one side, arms wrapped around herself, watching as several of the observers who had been sitting in on the trial filed out of the courtroom.

"What's happening?" Karen asked. She looked terrible. Eyes wide, with heavy bags visible through even heavier makeup. She'd clearly lost weight from even the first time she had testified. She was even trembling just a bit, despite her attempts to warm herself by rubbing her crossed arms with pale hands.

"I need to ask you a question," Talon told her, "and I need you to tell me the truth."

Karen took a moment, staring at Talon with those gaunt eyes. "Okay."

Talon wasn't convinced. "The truth," she repeated. "It has to be the truth. I don't care what you say, as long as it's true. Hunter isn't here; the guards won't let him out of the courtroom. Chad isn't here; I told him to stay put inside. It's just you. I have a decision to make. It's my decision. Just me. What you say to me doesn't go beyond us and when I make my decision, I won't tell anyone why. Do you understand me?"

Karen took a moment, then nodded. "I think so."

"Do you believe me?"

Karen took a longer moment. Finally, another nod. "Yes. I believe you."

"Okay, good." Talon nodded. "Are you ready? Are you ready to tell me the truth?"

Karen nodded again. "Yes."

Talon locked eyes with her. "What do you think should happen to Hunter for what he did to your parents?"

Karen's eyebrows shot up, and her eyes widened even more, stretching those exhaustion bags over the tops of her cheeks. Her mouth tightened, making her lips almost disappear into her mouth. And her neck flushed, red blotches reaching over her jawline. Talon suspected she had a ringing in her ears too.

"The truth," Talon reminded her.

Karen frowned, but her eyes never glistened. Not for Hunter anyway. And she answered Talon's question. "He should go to prison for the rest of his life."

Talon finally exhaled. She nodded. "You're right," she said. "And you can go home now."

* * *

Fifteen minutes later, Judge Kozlowski called the courtroom to order and repeated his invitation to Talon. "The defense may call its next witness."

Talon stood up. "We have no more witnesses, Your Honor. The defense rests."

It was all over but the closing arguments.

And the verdict. Always that verdict.

CHAPTER 44

With only a single witness in the defense case-in-chief, they had finished before noon. They could have returned after lunch for both the prosecution and defense closing arguments, but Riordan wanted a day 'to mull over the testimony of Mr. Jankles', and Talon didn't mind an extra twenty hours or so to work on her own closing. So, the judge called it an early day, again, and sent everyone home until the next morning at 9:00 a.m.

At 8:50 a.m. everyone was once again assembled in the courtroom, save the jurors in the jury room and the judge in his chambers. Talon walked over to the prosecution table. She could have leaned over from her seat, but she wanted to make sure Riordan could hear her too.

"Are you doing the closing, Cecilia?" Talon asked. "Since Ron did the opening?"

"Mr. Riordan will be doing the closing argument as well," Cecilia responded formally, to an approving nod from her supervisor. "He is lead counsel on it, after all."

"True," Talon conceded. "But I think it was smart to have a woman help out on the case. Men can be so emotional."

Men were in fact every bit as emotional as women but had

somehow sold a narrative that anger wasn't an emotion. And nothing made a man more emotional than telling him he was emotional.

Cecilia couldn't manage a response, primarily because she was trying not to laugh. Riordan had no trouble responding, though, and emotionally to boot. "Step away, Winter. Your client is going to pay for what he did, no matter what your whore expert says."

"You say 'whore' like it's a bad thing," Talon returned. "Another thing men get emotional about."

"Your mind games aren't going to work on us," Riordan sneered.

"Clearly," Talon laughed.

"I think we're done, Talon," Cecilia told her. Talon decided to take that as code for 'mission: accomplished'.

Talon returned to her seat, then the bailiff escorted the jury to the jury box, and Judge Kozlowski took the bench. Once everyone was seated and situated, the judge spoke.

"Ladies and gentlemen, please give your attention to Mr. Riordan, who will deliver closing argument on behalf of the State of Washington."

Riordan nodded up to the judge, ignored Talon, and took a spot directly in front of the jury box. He was probably half a step closer than he was for his opening statement. A half step too close. Talon noticed at least two jurors look over questioningly at Cecilia as Riordan came over to talk at them yet again.

"I told you at the beginning of the trial that this was an easy case," Riordan almost shouted, "and nothing that happened during the trial has changed that. Not stories about walks through the woods, or fantasies about doing unnecessary DNA testing, and certainly not half-qualified experts selling their opinions to the highest bidder."

Definitely not emotional, Talon thought with more than a little satisfaction.

"Let's just step back from the smoke and mirrors for a moment, shall we?" Riordan continued. "And remember what the evidence actually shows. Arnold and Florence Grovequist were brutally murdered in their own home. They tried to call 911 but the killer, the defendant, took the phone away so he could finish the job. Police were dispatched anyway. By the time they arrived, the defendant had finished the murders. The police, fearing the worst, broke down the door and found the defendant only a few feet away from the murder scene, holding the murder weapon, covered in the blood of the murder victims. That's easy. That's catching the murderer literally red-handed. That's a guilty verdict."

Riordan took a moment to catch his breath. He pushed a hand through his hair and let out a sigh.

"In the old days, back in England, there would be these things called fox hunts," he said. Talon knew where this was headed—she'd heard the spiel before from other prosecutors—but she was still surprised Riordan was going there. Entertained, but still surprised. "They would trap a fox and then on the day of the hunt, they would let it loose, and it would run away as fast as it could. Then the hunters would try to chase it down, using bloodhounds. The bloodhounds would follow the fox's scent and part of the event was seeing how good your dogs were."

A quick glance at the jury confirmed they had no idea what he was talking about, or why. At least Talon's weird, made up story was original.

"Well, one of the ways they tested the dogs," Riordan went on, "was to cut open fish and drag the bodies across the main pathway and into bushes. It was designed to trick the dogs and make them follow the fish's scent instead of the fox's. Those fish were herrings, and because they were cut open, they were bloody and red, and that's where we get the phrase 'red herring'. It means something worthless that's meant to trick you from your real goal.

"In this case the red herrings are those things the defense attorney kept bringing up," Riordan said. "Using a bat instead of your fists, testing a blood covered baseball bat to see if it has blood on it, a psychologist—not even a psychiatrist, just a psychologist—who agrees that the defendant's behavior is also consistent with being guilty. Those are all red herrings, designed to distract you from your real goal. But your real goal is justice, and I know you won't be diverted from its path."

Riordan stole a glance at Talon, but she was ready for it and flashed him a smile. He didn't seem to like that and spun his head back to face the jury.

"Look, if you want to believe that you should bother doing a DNA test on a murder weapon literally dripping in the victims' blood and still in the murderer's hand," he said, "or if you want to believe that the reason the defendant froze when the cops caught him wasn't because he just got caught but instead was some Sudden Onset Stress Disorder or whatever mental illness that so-called expert diagnosed, then fine, go ahead, believe that, and find him not guilty."

Talon's eyebrows shot up. It was probably not a good idea to dare the jury to acquit a defendant. Not good for Riordan, that is. It was great for her.

"But there's an old saying in the law," he continued, "when you hear hoofbeats, don't look for zebras."

Another tried and tired prosecution metaphor.

"In this case," Riordan explained, "the hoofbeats are the mountain of evidence against the defendant, the zebras are what the defense wants you to think might have happened despite all of that evidence, and the horses are the truth. You know it's horses. You know it's the truth. And you know to find the defendant guilty. Thank you."

Riordan spun on his heel and marched back to his seat next to Cecilia. She congratulated him, but her heart didn't seem to be in it.

"What the hell was he talking about?" Hunter whispered to Talon.

"I'm not entirely sure," Talon answered. "But it doesn't matter."

"Now, ladies and gentlemen," Judge Kozlowski called out, "please give your attention to Ms. Winter who will deliver the closing argument on behalf of the defendant."

CHAPTER 45

Talon took up a similar spot to where Riordan had stood, but rather than a half-step too close, she was maybe a half-step too far away. She wanted to engage their intellects, not stir their emotions. She was a professor, not a drill sergeant.

"I'm glad Mr. Riordan has embraced my metaphor of walking the path of justice," she began, "but I don't think he quite gets it. But that's okay, because I'm pretty sure you all do."

Everyone liked a compliment.

"I'm going to take us all down that path again," Talon continued, "but before I do, there are a few things that are very important to remember. The first of those is that the government is the one who accused a private citizen of a crime. When they do that, they have the burden of proving the crime beyond a reasonable doubt. That means they have to prove each and every element of the crime beyond a reasonable doubt. So, if they prove four out of five elements beyond a reasonable doubt, you vote not guilty. If they prove ninety-nine out of a hundred elements beyond a reasonable doubt, you vote not guilty. Not only do you vote not guilty, you have a *duty* to vote not guilty. It's your oath, your sacred charge, and I know you didn't answer your summons at the beginning of this trial only to violate your oath at the end of it."

She jerked a thumb toward Riordan and Cecilia. "Prosecutors love that story about the red herrings. I don't even know if it's true that that's where we get the word from. That's another red herring maybe. But see, what they love about it, is that it suggests if you take the time to look into anything other than what they want you to look at, that it's somehow a waste of time, that you've somehow been tricked. But really, if there's something that pulls you off their path, that means they didn't prove that part of their case. And the last thing they want you to be thinking back there in the jury room when you start your deliberations is all the reasons why you couldn't stay on the path they tried to keep you on."

Talon seemed to be getting looks of understanding, maybe even agreement, from at least a few of the jurors.

"Which brings me to the second very important thing to remember as we look at the evidence in this case," Talon continued. "All of the evidence in this case, everything you heard, everything you saw, all of it—that was the State's evidence. The only witness we called was a psychologist who examined Hunter because there was no way the State was going to look into, let alone document mental health issues that might benefit him. You heard what Detective Tomlinson told you: there was no need to look into the actual evidence in the case; they were done investigating in that first three seconds when they saw Hunter and then tackled him to the ground.

"But ladies and gentlemen, if there's a so-called red herring pulling you off the chosen path, that's their red herring. I didn't put it there. They did. Every piece of evidence I'm about to discuss came from their witnesses, not mine. It's their evidence. Their own evidence pulls you off their path. And it's their own evidence that prevents you from getting across that chasm between the presumption of innocence, where we stand now, and guilty by proof beyond a reasonable doubt, on the far, far other side."

That was a very important point, and the one that ultimately led Talon to not call Karen Burgess to the stand a second time. A defense attorney wasn't allowed to lie to a jury, but they could argue possible theories of the case that were supported by the prosecution's own evidence. If she put Karen on the stand, then whatever Karen said would be Talon's evidence, and Talon would be limited in arguing anything untrue from it. But if the State put on evidence that supported a particular theory that a defendant was innocent, not only could the defense attorney argue that theory knowing their client was guilty, they were ethically obligated to do so. There were appellate cases directly on point, cases where convictions were reversed because defense attorneys refused to argue things they knew were false but were nevertheless supported by the prosecution's evidence. It was that kind of stuff that led people at parties to ask, 'How can you do that job?'

Talon knew Hunter did it. She also knew the State left enough holes in their case that an alternate explanation of the crime had bubbled to the surface, barely perceptible to any but the best. But it wasn't just that she could make the argument she was about to make. She was professionally required to.

It was her duty.

"Let's go through the evidence, their evidence," Talon said, "and let's see if we can put more thought into it than the three seconds Sergeant Unker took to tackle Hunter Burgess, and the zero seconds it took Detective Tomlinson not to order any forensic tests that might have shed additional light on what really happened in that house that night."

She raised a finger to start her countdown of the evidence.

"First, the person who did this used a baseball bat. A weapon. Something over and above what a man Hunter's size and age would have needed. Their own medical examiner testified that blunt force trauma caused by the fists and feet of someone like Hunter would have been more than enough to cause the deaths of his elderly grandmother and grandfather.

"Second, there was an opportunity to determine exactly who swung that bat that night by examining the DNA on it, not to mention elsewhere in the crime scene, but the State failed to do that.

"Third, Hunter had no motive to murder his grandparents. For one thing, Detective Tomlinson himself described Hunter's designated inheritance as small. For another, he couldn't collect it anyway as the murderer. It would revert to his mom, as the only surviving heir.

"Fourth, Hunter stayed at his grandparents' home sometimes. He even had a bed there. But his mother thought he wasn't there very often. So, he was probably there more often than she realized."

"Fifth, the police didn't contact Karen Burgess until hours after the murders.

"And finally, when the police discovered Hunter inside the home, he didn't try to run away, or fight the cops, or do anything other than get tackled and handcuffed and taken away."

Talon stepped over to the defense table and gestured lightly at her client. "Those are not the actions of a murderer. Those are the actions of a grandson who was the first person to discover his murdered grandparents. Yes, it was our witness, Dr. Jankles, who explained that, but his diagnosis was based on what the State's own witnesses said and did that night."

She stepped back in front of the jurors. "The State's evidence simply does not support their theory that Hunter Burgess killed his grandparents. It supports that his mother, Karen Burgess, did it."

Talon stopped and surveyed the courtroom. The jurors seemed surprised, but attentive, even interested. Riordan looked shocked. Cecilia looked worried. Karen Burgess looked broken. Her husband next to her looked hopeful. And Judge Kozlowski had his hand over the lower half of his face, but his eyes looked impressed.

Talon turned back to the jurors. "I'm not saying that Karen Burgess murdered her own parents for money, using a weapon to do it because she couldn't do it with her bare hands. I'm not saying that unknown to her, Hunter was in the grandparents' house, and so he heard the commotion and came out to find them murdered. I'm not saying that he got himself covered in blood when he threw himself on their bodies and tried to save them. I'm not saying he picked up the murder weapon and took it with him when he staggered out of his grandparent's bedroom so it couldn't be used on him. I'm not saying the police barged in and tackled the wrong man, who the American Psychiatric Association says was acting exactly like a person who had just found his grandparents murdered. I'm not saying the police jumped to the wrong conclusion and the prosecutors jumped right after them

"I'm not saying any of that."

She pointed at the prosecutors. "Their own evidence says that. All of that."

She turned back to the jurors.

"Did Karen Burgess really murder her own parents and leave her son to take the fall for it?" she asked. "Maybe, maybe not. But that maybe means you don't know either. It means the evidence supports that theory as much or more as the fish story Mr. Riordan told you. That means there's doubt. Reasonable doubt. And that means there is one and only one verdict possible in this case.

"Not guilty.

"Thank you."

The courtroom was silent for a moment. Then the silence was broken by the sobs of Karen Burgess, sitting in the gallery, her head in her hands, her husband's unsure arm hovering over, but not quite on her back.

No one, not even the judge, dared say anything for a few moments. Then Karen stood up and ran out of the courtroom. Chad hesitated, then followed after, but at a slow plod. The room was electric. Talon couldn't feel her hands for the tingling. Somehow Hunter knew not to try to say a damn thing to her. Everyone waited. Until finally the judge found his voice again.

"Ladies and gentlemen of the jury," he croaked, "that concludes the trial. You will now retire to the jury room to begin your deliberations." Then he cleared his throat and quoted from the final jury instruction for criminal cases. "As jurors, you are officers of this court. You must not let your emotions overcome your rational thought process. You must reach your decision based on the facts proved to you, not on sympathy, prejudice, or personal preference. To assure that all parties receive a fair trial, you must act impartially with an earnest desire to reach a proper verdict."

What was a proper verdict anyway?

Talon wasn't even sure anymore.

CHAPTER 46

Deliberations could take days, even weeks. Generally speaking, the longer the better for the defense. Quick verdicts meant the jurors were unanimous and convinced, and that meant a conviction. Slower verdicts meant someone was holding out, or they weren't sure about something. And if they weren't sure, they were supposed to acquit. At least, that was the theory.

Talon returned to her office and tried to decide whether she could actually manage to do any work that afternoon. She certainly didn't expect to be interrupted by a call from Kozlowski's bailiff, but she was wiped out. Trial work was draining. But if she wasn't completely drained, had she really done her best?

She opened her email for the first time in forever. Among the deluge was a plea from Cassandra Sondheim to please call her with a decision. And a days-old invitation from Jeff Rodgers which just reminded Talon had already missed Patty's memorial service.

Then the phone rang.

It was Judge Kozlowski's bailiff.

The jury had reached a verdict.

That was fast. Too fast. *Damn.*

They must have come to that proper verdict after all.

CHAPTER 47

The reading of the verdict seemed to take as long as the entire rest of the trial put together. It didn't, of course, but time moved slower as everyone assembled for the conclusion of the colossal personal and professional endeavor that was a murder trial. Double murder trial.

Talon was the first to arrive. She took her seat at the defense table. Rather than binders full of reports and research, she had brought a single legal pad, and that only so she could have something, anything, on the table in front of her.

Cecilia and Riordan arrived next. Riordan was smiling ear to ear. He knew what a quick verdict meant, too, especially when two grandparents had been bludgeoned in their bed. Cecilia managed a neutral expression, but she avoided eye contact with Talon. Riordan didn't.

"Quick verdict, huh?" he gloated. "When do you want to schedule the sentencing hearing? I mean, assuming it's a guilty verdict, of course," he added belatedly.

"Why don't we just wait to see what the verdict actually is," Talon suggested.

"Okay, okay." Riordan chucked and raised his hands

defensively at her. "No need to get emotional."

Any response Talon might have shot back at him was interrupted by the sound of the side door opening and Hunter being escorted into the courtroom by two uniformed jail guards.

"That was quick," he said to Talon after being pushed into the seat next to her. "Is that good?"

Talon shook her head. "No."

"Oh," Hunter said. "Well, that's too bad."

Talon agreed. Mostly. At least she could feel good that she really had given it her all. She just thought they'd be out longer. She must not have given them as much to think about as she thought she had.

The door from the hallway opened and Talon turned around to see Chad Burgess walk in. Karen wasn't with him. Talon didn't suppose she could blame her. The door opened again and in walked Curt. He gave her a smile and thumbs-up, then took a seat in the back. Support.

Talon smiled slightly and turned back to face the front of the courtroom. The bailiff and the court reporter were already at their stations below the judge's bench. With everyone assembled, the bailiff picked up the phone and whispered into it. A minute later, Judge Kozlowski emerged from his chambers and took the bench.

"The jury has informed us that they have reached a verdict," he announced. "Are there any matters to be addressed before we bring them in to announce their verdicts?"

Talon had nothing. Neither did the State.

"So be it," the judge said. "Bring them in."

The bailiff crossed to the jury room and summoned the jurors into the jury box. They filed in and took their seats.

"Will the presiding juror please stand?" Kozlowski instructed.

A middle-aged man in a burgundy sweater stood up, two pieces of paper in his hand.

"Has the jury reached a verdict?" the judge asked.

"We have," the presiding juror responded.

"Please hand the verdict forms to the bailiff," Kozlowski directed.

The juror did as he was told, and the bailiff in turn walked the verdict forms to the judge. Talon watched intently and was always amazed that the bailiffs never even tried to sneak a peek at what the jury had decided. The judge accepted the verdict forms and read them to himself, keeping a perfect poker face as he did so. He looked up.

"Will the defendant please rise?"

Hunter looked at Talon and she nodded. He stood up for the reading of the verdict. She stood up too.

"In the matter of *The State of Washington versus Hunter Burgess*," Judge Kozlowski read aloud from the first of the two verdict forms, "as to count one, murder in the first degree, we the jury find the defendant..."

Talon closed her eyes and exhaled. She'd done her best.

"...not guilty."

Talon's eyes flew open. She looked at Hunter for confirmation that she'd actually heard what she thought she'd just heard. He didn't look back at her, but the giant smile exploding on his face was confirmation enough.

Kozlowski moved to the second verdict form, but it could hardly be a different result. "In the matter of *The State of Washington versus Hunter Burgess*, as to count two, murder in the first degree, we the jury find the defendant not guilty."

Talon's gaze raced around the courtroom. Cecilia's head was hanging. Riordan slammed the table and stormed toward the exit, leaving Cecilia behind even as court was still in session. Chad was smiling. Curt was too. And Hunter?

Hunter pumped his fists into the air. "I did it!" he shouted. "And I got away with it!"

EPILOGUE

'Patricia Little Rodgers.'
'Wife, Mother, Advocate.'

The years on the gravestone didn't matter. She was born alone, and she died alone.

Life has no meaning.

Talon set a single yellow rose on the granite and walked away. It was cloudy, but not overcast. There was a breeze, but it wasn't too cold. She pulled her phone from her pocket and dialed.

So, you make your own meaning.

"Hello? This is Talon Winter. I think I'm ready to try civil practice again," she said. "Yes. The Commencement Bay Yacht Club case. Let's take our fucking land back."

END

THE TALON WINTER LEGAL THRILLERS
Winter's Law
Winter's Chance
Winter's Reason
Winter's Justice
Winter's Duty

THE DAVID BRUNELLE LEGAL THRILLERS
Presumption of Innocence
Tribal Court
By Reason of Insanity
A Prosecutor for the Defense
Substantial Risk
Corpus Delicti
Accomplice Liability
A Lack of Motive
Missing Witness
Diminished Capacity
Devil's Plea Bargain
Homicide in Berlin
Premeditated Intent

ALSO BY STEPHEN PENNER
Scottish Rite
Blood Rite
Last Rite
Mars Station Alpha
The Godling Club

ABOUT THE AUTHOR

Stephen Penner is an attorney, author, and artist from Seattle.

In addition to writing the *Talon Winter Legal Thrillers*, he is also the author of the *David Brunelle Legal Thriller Series*, starring Seattle homicide prosecutor David Brunelle; the *Maggie Devereaux Paranormal Mysteries*, recounting the exploits of an American graduate student in the magical Highlands of Scotland; and several stand-alone works.

For more information, please visit *www.stephenpenner.com*.